Hell's Grannies:

Kickass Tales of the Crone

Edited by April Grey

Published by Lafcadio Press
New York City

D1713202

Women may be the one group
that grows more radical with age.

-Gloria Steinem

Contents

INTRODUCTION
HELL'S GRANNIES:
KICKASS TALES OF THE CRONE

What a Drag It is Getting Old...
"Mother's Little Helper,"
The Rolling Stones

I had always planned to age gracefully. Achieving motherhood at forty, in spite of an undiagnosed autoimmune disease, put a crimp into that plan. Now entering my cronehood, I'm grateful just to get out of bed in the morning.

Aging is not for the faint-hearted, yet there is little choice in the matter. You can take good care of your health, your finances, your loved ones and still life will throw a curve ball.

In this anthology you will find tales of courage, of women who rise to the challenges of time in many different ways.

Some stories are of women aging gracefully but their tales are still kickass because they have a lot to overcome. Other stories are humorous, because if you can't age gracefully, then by all means age disgracefully. Remember the Monty Python sketch of Hell's Grannies or Jenny Joseph's poem, "When I am Old I shall wear Purple?" They were in my mind when I chose these stories. Humor may be the best tonic and part of the wisdom of the Crone.

And there are a couple of very dark tales as well. I think you will delight in them as much as I do.

Finally, four of the authors in this anthology are British and one is Australian—I chose to retain the flavor of their native lands by *not* Americanizing their spelling and grammar. So if you come across color spelled as colour, it is not a typo.

The authors have all given wonderful interpretations of what it means to be a Hell's Granny and I hope you will take the time to engage them on social media and read more of their work.

Looking forward to hearing from you, don't be shy and leave a review!

April Grey, NYC December, 2015

The inspiration for this story comes from the poem, "Eurydice" by Ann Duffy.

Eurydice
By Patricia Cochrane

As we walked the cliffs, he talked enthusiastically of the wonderful future he had planned with his young fiancée.

"Once you and I are divorced I hardly need tell you how impatient I shall be to start a family. You have always known how much I desired to have children and how devastating it was for me that you were never able to get pregnant." He sighs heavily. "I would be dishonest if I denied the relief I felt when the fertility tests gave me the all clear. You understand I know."

"Of course," I murmur and notice how especially beautiful this evening is, the sky a delicate grey, cumulus clouds collecting low on the horizon.

"I appreciate how much you love 'doing art' as they say, but unfortunately I shall no longer be able to finance your freedom to paint." He links his arm in mine. "It was so fortuitous that long ago you gave up your art studies to teach; now you can go back to teaching and be an independent woman!"

The Westerly wind is playful; gulls ride the breeze, allowing themselves to be carried back inland. He fails to mention that I gave up my much-loved art training to support him as a struggling young actor. Perhaps he's forgotten? Though I doubt that, he has an excellent memory.

He enthuses, "There is no reason why you should not marry again, have a fresh start, perhaps even adopt." He stops and turns my face to his. "You are after all only fifty-six and quite an attractive woman. The world is your oyster." His voice is warm, musical.

Smiling at his words, I continue walking. I know from long experience that he has no interest in my responses. I love these cliffs, where undergrowth hides the ugly erosion scars.

We sit on the bench where long ago, we composed memorial plaques to each other. He shows me the divorce settlement his solicitor had drawn up. I take his proffered pen and duly sign.

"But you haven't read it!" he exclaims as I hand the papers back to him.

I have no need to. I know by signing it I would forfeit my rights to the country house, the London apartment, the holiday cottage, his considerable wealth.

"Here, read the agreement do." Anxiously he thrusts the document at me.

I know him so well. "I'd rather you read to me." What actor can resist the request for oration? He clears his throat, (an affectation), as we continue our walk along the narrow path.

"A moment." I touch his arm. "Change places do, otherwise the wind will blow your words away."

He flashes his heartbreaking smile as I move from the cliff-edge.

His beautiful voice enunciates perfectly all my losses. He reads it like a poem, a poem of betrayal, meanness, dismissal. We approach the spot where the cliff had recently fallen, a ghastly open wound that had taken some of the path with it.

"I love listening to you, even if I don't like what you're saying."

He inclines his head in appreciation of my admiration. "I always maintain content isn't of importance; delivery is everything."

The words rise and fall with melodious elegance. If I closed my eyes and listened to the rhythm, it might be a declaration of love.

I stoop as if to remove a stone from my shoe. He, not realizing I had stopped, continues to walk, still reading. "I missed that bit. Please read it again," I implore him.

"But of course." He turns to face me, repeating what he supposes I missed. The wonderfully rounded vowels and crisp clear consonants float into the air, and there they hang, as he steps backwards into the void. A wordless shout, then…silence.

I reach up my hand as the wind returns the agreement to me. Was this how Eurydice felt? I wonder.

Patricia Cochrane: On retirement I moved to Hastings and joined a writers group. I had always been a prolific reader but this was the first time, apart from school essays, I had tried writing and I love it. I divide my time between London, where my children and grandchildren live and Hastings where I garden, walk, practice Ti Chi and spend time with friends. I had trained and practised as a psychotherapist and this influences much of my writing.

"The Pensioner Pirates of Marine Parade" is my one and only Science Fiction story. I based it in St Leonards on Sea as people use their mobility scooters, sometimes at speed, to drive along the front. Suppose in the future they went on the water? And suppose some of these people, especially the elderly, were fighting for their lives? Clarissa and Daphne emerged as feisty individuals who use any means possible, both practical and fantastic, to put up a fight against bureaucracy. -JB

The Pensioner Pirates of Marine Parade
By Jonathan Broughton

"Look sharp Daphne, Hugo Marshall's arrived." Clarissa reversed her mobility scooter away from the window. "Now remember, don't say anything and look blank."

Daphne gazed into space. In a world of her own, thought Clarissa. Looking blank was as natural to her as breathing, though that had been a bit ragged these last few days.

"Follow me," Clarissa ordered and she trundled out of her flat and headed for the lift with Daphne close behind.

The main reception was packed, mostly with young or middle aged relatives who had elderly relations living in Marine Parade. Vultures, thought Clarissa as she eased her scooter behind the throng. Out to make a few quid from the misfortunes of the old. Just you wait till you're in your hundreds and need help - then I bet euthanasia won't be high on your list of priorities.

She spotted a few other pensioners, the hopeless cases, those with extreme dementia who didn't know the difference between day and night, no doubt dragged out to illustrate government policy.

She parked behind a wall of bodies close to the stage. A good spot, she could hear and if she leant to the left or right just see the stage. Daphne drew alongside and bumped a couple as she manoeuvred into position. They turned, angry and shocked, though when they saw Daphne and her clumsy steering they shook their heads and rolled their eyes in resigned despair.

A ripple of applause and the crowd hushed to silence.

"Good morning, everyone." Hugo Marshall, Hastings Mayor and Clarissa ground her teeth. He shone in the spotlight like an oily fish. His bald head gleamed, his grey tailored suit glistened, his black patent leather shoes twinkled and his wide smile beamed.

"I didn't expect to see so many of you here," he began.

Clarissa snorted. Really? Every street corner in Hastings, every lamppost, had been plastered with posters.

"Today," Hugo Marshall continued, "I am happy to announce that The Silver Dusk will be sailing into Hastings on Monday the 20th October."

An appreciative murmur from the crowd and the couple in front of Clarissa turned to each other and smiled.

Hugo Marshall's voice adopted a considerate tone. "Do you have an elderly relative ready to die? Are you struggling financially to meet their upkeep?" Then, more strident. "Are you tired of resources being

14

squandered on members of society no longer able to look after themselves? Inconsiderate individuals who took advantage of medical breakthroughs in the first two decades of this century to prolong their lives, but didn't consider the means needed to support their advancing years and now rely on you for their care and well-being?"

A chorus of assent rumbled around the room. "I thought so."

Clarissa wanted to smash her fist into his smug face.

"Well," he went on, "the expert team on The Silver Dusk can help. No funeral expenses, no costly cemetery upkeep. Do you know, and I speak from personal experience here, they are wonderful." His voice went low, almost husky. "My mother was so grateful when I took her on board. She was a burden, emotionally and financially, to the family and of course to the country. She understood that and chose the correct course of action. I shall never forget that last happy evening," his voice cracked and a single tear slid down his cheek, "sitting in their Starlight Suite playing Scrabble. The lovely attentive staff helped mother choose the letters and the memory of those final wonderful hours lingered when we came to say our goodbyes the next day." He took a deep breath. "Do you know, they even let us float the paper bag with her ashes out to sea."

A whispered 'ah' rose from the crowd.

Bloody bastard, thought Clarissa. I'd give him triple word score with bells on!

Hugo Marshall cleared his throat. "Look around you, see the hopeless, helpless ravages of old age. These poor souls are incapable of making the right decision, but you, you can ease their pain. Join me at mid-day on

The Silver Dusk and help your loved ones sail away to a golden sunset. The first five customers will receive a thousand pounds cash."

Applause greeted his promise of money, but he hadn't quite finished and the crowd went silent as he delivered his final line.

"I care about the elderly. Do you?"

There were cheers and whoops of approval. Clarissa glanced at Daphne and smirked.

Clarissa steered her mobility scooter into the sea. "Look sharp Daphne," she called. "Operation ROPES is a go!"

She glanced in her side mirror to watch Daphne drive down the concrete breakwater. As the front wheels of her scooter splashed into the surf she applied the aqua lever and the air cushion inflated as the fan booster whirred into life behind her seat.

Clarissa banked sharp right to line up beside her friend and breast astern, they bobbed up and down on the swell.

"Have you remembered to bring everything?" Clarissa asked. Daphne's memory slipped a lot nowadays, or chose random moments to be selective. Today's operation required concentration and keen wits. One error might find them belly-up in the briny.

Daphne un-clipped the bright red plastic picnic-hamper in her front basket and peered at the contents.

"Checklist," announced Clarissa. "Faces?"

Daphne held up two latex masks, gross caricatures of old men with huge warty noses, tufts of long white curly hair and cauliflower ears.

16

"Pistols?"

Daphne grunted as she lifted the yellow and pink fluorescent water guns, moulded as AK47 rifles, into her arms.

"Loaded?" queried Clarissa, though Daphne's red face as she cradled them against her chest made it pretty obvious. Still, Daphne squeezed the yellow one's trigger and a jet of water shot across the sea and sent a paddling seagull skywards with a loud squawk.

"Good girl," congratulated Clarissa. "And ROPES?"

Daphne dumped the water pistols and slid two short poles wound with black velvet out of the bottom of the picnic hamper. She unfurled one to reveal a skull and crossbones and the slogan Respect Our PEnsionerS emblazoned across it in bright red darning wool.

"Perfect," Clarissa purred.

The sea mist rolled over them and onto the shore in waves of moisture. No breeze and no sign of the mist thinning. It never cleared, not since the earth had warmed up and melted the ice caps. The sun glowed like a yellow metal disc that gave no warmth and very little light. The calm grey water might be ice it was so smooth. Excellent conditions for piratical exploits.

"Give me one of them, dear," ordered Clarissa.

Daphne handed her one of the flags and she slotted it into the right hand mirror bracket. Daphne copied her and they were almost set.

"Synchronise watches." Clarissa rolled up her cardigan sleeve. "Eleven twenty five precisely."

Daphne's watch slipped upside down on her bony wrist and Clarissa reached across and helped her twist it back.

"It's hard to tell what that says," Clarissa grumbled. A grinning portrait of Hugo Marshall filled the watch face, "An air-brushed ear lobe past a piggy eye. Well, it looks near enough, it'll have to do."

She checked her battery charge dial, the arrow flickered just under full. She glanced across at Daphne's, which looked identical. Now that the time for action had arrived, her stomach tingled.

"All right dear. Now, The Silver Dusk is moored just off the old pier. Hugo Marshall is due to leave the harbour at eleven forty five. We need to get into position between The Silver Dusk and the harbour."

This was their most audacious pirate attack yet. The thought of all that lovely money fired Clarissa's enthusiasm which she tempered with moral sensibilities.

"We're doing this for Hugo Marshall's mother," she announced. "We didn't know her, but she didn't deserve to die. Come on Daphne, raise anchor and Yo Ho Ho and a bottle of rum!"

She engaged her gear lever and eased in the accelerator. The fan booster whined and the scooter slid across the water. The flag unfurled and flapped as she picked up speed.

"Stay beside me," she called. She didn't want to lose Daphne in the fog and the wake from her scooter might bounce her out of her seat.

The old pier's rusty legs loomed out of the mist to her left, a red light blinked on the last piece of twisted metal, an excellent pointer to keep them on track and she pushed her accelerator to maximum. Poor old pier. She remembered the fire that destroyed it in 2010 and the earthquake of 2030 that tipped the remains into the sea. All that fuss about re-building had been a waste of time and money. What had happened to all that money? Nobody said.

The arrow on the compass next to the battery dial wobbled as it hovered over South.

"No room for error dear," she called. "We're on our own now. Due south until we bump into The Silver Dusk and then north east towards the harbour."

The fan's whirr sounded so loud in the murky silence. The sea slapped against the inflated cushions; she and Daphne might be the only people on earth. The fog provided excellent cover, though it could prove treacherous if they steered off course.

Clarissa shuddered. Each year during bad weather pensioners went missing, presumed swept out to sea, after the earthquake opened the ravine that split Hastings in two. Tragic tales of mobility scooters spotted floating in the shipping lanes that criss-crossed the English Channel, their batteries dead and more often than not, their occupants too. To attempt a rescue was never contemplated, one less mouth to feed, one less expense for upkeep. It took pensioners like her and Daphne to make a stand against the authorities. TAR, she thought, Third Age Revolts, good acronym for partisan activities.

"Look sharp Daphne." She decreased the accelerator and her scooter slowed.

A dark mass loomed before them, as high as a cliff and as solid as a wall. Clarissa's heart thumped, The Silver Dusk, the death ship. No portholes broke its uniform bulk and thick fog obscured its upper decks. Silent and still, even the sea had turned a darker shade of grey.

She signalled left with her arm. She didn't dare speak because a horrid thought that, somehow, this floating executioner might be watching, kept her silent.

Then, with a blast that sent her nerves into orbit and the dreaded horror that her fears had been realised, the ship's foghorn shattered the silence with one long boom. If death had a voice, this might be it and she whimpered with shock.

Daphne's scooter collided into her and sent them both into a spin. They circled like wasps trapped in a jam-jar of water, until Clarissa reached across and yanked Daphne's accelerator off. They drifted away from The Silver Dusk, until it was little more than a huge smudge in the fog.

Clarissa breathed deep to quieten her nerves. Her ears pounded with rushing blood, which to her alarm increased in volume. She held her breath, it wasn't her ears, the sound came from all directions; the deep throb of a powerful engine as it churned through the water.

Flee, her mind screamed, but which way? Any direction might be wrong. Daphne's blank face gazed at her as she waited for instructions. Clarissa peered into the fog and her scooter trembled as it vibrated with the building noise.

The fog swirled and parted between them and The Silver Dusk and a golden motor-boat, high-prowed and sleek, slid past in a majestic sweep before the fog closed in and obscured it once more. The wash rolled towards them and sent them careering up and down, as sick-making as the worst rollercoaster.

"That's the boat that takes the victims to the death ship," Clarissa whispered when she had recovered her breath. "Thank goodness it didn't spot us. You all right dear? That was a nasty shock."

Daphne's tiny hands glowed white as she gripped her scooter's handles.

"It's off to the harbour for its first pick-up," Clarissa reasoned and then a terrible thought popped into her head. "I do hope Hugo Marshall doesn't come back on board. It's too big for us to tackle. I didn't think of that. Oh well, we'll have to wait and see." She laid a hand on her friend's arm. "Be prepared to abort the mission if I tell you to, dear."

She engaged the reverse gear and dis-entangled herself from Daphne. The compass needle trembled as the scooter completed a slow circle and lined up pointing north-east.

"Back on course," confirmed Clarissa. "Off we go."

She didn't know how far they might need to travel, just as long as they were out of visible range of The Silver Dusk and the harbour wall. She checked her watch, eleven forty.

"Two more minutes," she announced, "and we'll be in position." The fog horn boomed once more and she jumped with fright.

"For goodness sakes," she growled. "If the lethal injection doesn't get you, stand next to that and you'll be scared to death."

Daphne's blank face registered surprised concentration. Bit like a worried sheep, thought Clarissa. I do hope she's up for this.

The fog seemed if anything thicker. Her hair and face were soaked with damp and her palms slipped on the scooter's plastic handles. She checked her watch again.

21

"Ten seconds," she called and slowed the scooter to a gentle three kilometres-an-hour. The digital seconds flicked by. "Three, two, one, stop!"

She engaged the gear to neutral and the fan wound down and clicked to a halt. Daphne's scooter slid across the water and with a gentle bump, lined up next to hers.

"Open the hamper," Clarissa instructed. "Have the masks handy, but we won't put them on till we know what we're up against." Daphne handed her one. "If that big gold boat comes back, turn round and head out to sea until it passes."

Daphne angled the water pistols with their hilts uppermost for a quick and easy draw.

"Just typical if Marshall decides to show off and travel in style," worried Clarissa. "Hey up – what was that?" She listened hard. "Do you hear it?" she whispered.

A gentle 'phut, phut, phut' echoed through the fog.

"I think we're in luck, my love." Clarissa grinned. "He's coming out in his fishing boat, just as I hoped." The inboard motor came closer.

"Masks on," she ordered. The cold latex stuck to her wet face and the rubber smell made her wince. She pushed the mask's bushy eyebrows out of the eye sockets, next time she would give them a good trim. She grabbed hold of the pink water pistol and laid it across her lap and then patted Daphne's hand.

"Quick in and quick out, remember?" The leering old man that faced her nodded.

Clarissa engaged the gear, gave a thumbs-up and eased the accelerator to maximum. The scooter shot forwards and the flag streamed beside her like running water.

Within seconds the tiny fishing boat jumped out of the fog in front of them.

"Avast there, you scurvy dog!" yelled Clarissa. She swerved to the right and Daphne swerved to the left.

Clarissa locked her knees under the scooter's handles, picked up the water pistol and pumped rapid jets of water across the boat's deck as she swept past. Daphne repeated the action on the opposite side.

Hugo Marshall, easy to spot in his scarlet regalia and gold chain of office, jumped up and attempted to shield his robes from the soaking by raising his hands as if he might push the water back.

Clarissa cleared the stern the same time as Daphne. She gripped the scooter's handle with one hand and yanked it sharp left. A quick glance behind her confirmed that Daphne had remembered what to do as she turned sharp right.

Lined up on opposite sides off the boat, they made another pass. Jets of water arched through the fog and Hugo Marshall's hands waved and flapped as one demented.

"Give us the money," shrieked Clarissa.

Through the boat's cabin window, a young man's face glowed green. Law dictated that all vehicles, except mobility scooters, be fitted with sat navs and to Clarissa's knowledge every single one of them shone with a green light. The man's eyes stared in wide disbelief at what was happening and as she and Daphne swept past for a third attack, the boat's speed decreased until it sat and wallowed in the swell left by their scooters.

"Pincers," Clarissa shouted as she aimed her scooter in a direct line at the boat's port side. Daphne did the same on the starboard side.

"Give us the money, Marshall." Clarissa heaved the pistol onto her shoulder, squinted through the plastic telescopic lens, which had no glass but two bits of bent wire for the crosshairs, and hit the Mayor with a faceful of water. He cursed and spluttered and his obscenities carried across the water. Daphne aimed for the back of his head. Spray rebounded in a dazzling display, like a glistening halo.

Clarissa's scooter bumped against the boat's side. There, at Hugo Marshall's feet was a large metal case. It gleamed with a silver shine. The money!

"Hand it over," she commanded and squirted his drenched face with another burst.

The young man slipped and slithered out of the cabin.

"Do something," gurgled Hugo Marshall.

Daphne focused her aim on the floundering youngster and he lost his footing and crashed face first into the bottom of the boat.

"Give it to me," Clarissa growled. "Or by Davy Jones's locker you'll take a swim with the fishes." Water sloshed in little wavelets around the Mayor's feet. He raised one arm to protect his face and with the other reached under his sodden robes.

"Keep your hands where I can see them," Clarissa shouted and pumped his chest in a series of staccato bursts. Daphne left off drenching the young man and copied Clarissa's tactics on the Mayor's back. The power of their ferocious bursts, the weight of his soaking robes and the waterlogged boards underfoot, unbalanced Hugo Marshall and he crumpled in a scarlet heap like a burst balloon.

As he fell, his foot kicked the metal box and sent it aquaplaning towards Clarissa. She stood up, leant over the scooter's handlebars and hooked the box's handle with the barrel of her water pistol. It was hers, all that lovely money and she dropped the box into her basket.

"Scatter," she called to Daphne as she engaged the scooter's reverse gear and drew away from the boat. Daphne looked up, as lost and wondering as a lonely child. Clarissa's heart sank. Not now Daphne, don't blank out now.

"Engage Daphne," she shrieked. "Scatter, scatter."

Daphne watched without the slightest flicker of awareness as the young man lurched to his feet. In his hands was a rope and attached to the end of the rope was a large hook.

"Get out of it Daphne." Clarissa flicked into forward gear and swerved towards the boat's stern.

With a loud clunk, the man hooked Daphne's handlebars and pulled the rope tight. The noise, or perhaps the man's close proximity, jumped Daphne out of her stupor and her booster fan whirred as she pulled away.

The man braced his feet against the boat's side as the rope tautened. His face strained with the effort of holding on, but the rope slipped through his hands and he let go with a loud yelp.

Daphne's scooter jumped back with a splash. Clarissa closed with her and reached for the hook, but Daphne engaged forward gear and accelerated away.

"Daphne, the hook, get rid of the hook," and she chased after her friend. What was she doing? She'd be tipped into the sea when the rope played out its length.

"Slow down," she yelled. Daphne's bent little figure hunched over the handlebars and her speed increased.

She swerved in front of the boat's prow and sped past port side towards the stern. She swerved again, up the starboard side and the trailing rope, slicing through the water with a hiss, wound round the boat.

Clarissa gave up giving chase, going round in circles made her dizzy and when Daphne shot past she saw, in her eyes, a look so grim that it made her gasp. Daphne's mind was clearly fixed on one thing, though what that might be Clarissa couldn't guess.

The young man crawled into the cabin. The lurid green glowed on his face as zombie flesh in a horror film might look. The boat's engine sputtered as he gunned it into life and then it whined with a high-pitched squeal, followed by a loud clank as it cut out.

Clarissa chortled. Daphne had jammed the propeller with the rope. Clever girl! Now she could clear the hook and leave Hugo Marshall stranded at sea.

Daphne decreased speed and turned her scooter to face the boat. She went into reverse and the rope tightened, wringing water drops into the sea. She glanced at the instruments on her handlebars and as Clarissa watched, she lined up in the direction of The Silver Dusk.

"Daphne?"

The fan booster whirred to full acceleration and Daphne moved backwards into the fog, her face beaming with joy and the fishing boat followed, slowly picking up speed.

Clarissa's scooter rocked in the gentle swell. She suddenly felt very lonely out on the ocean; her victory over Hugo Marshall, hollow, almost worthless. In fact everything was pointless, because when she thought about it, everyone died and whether it was helped along by a smiling nurse with a lethal injection or the carelessness of being carried out to sea in bad weather, didn't matter. Death happened, happy, sad or ordered. It took courage to make a deliberate choice and she marvelled at Daphne's resolve. She didn't think the old girl had it in her.

Her maudlin thoughts evaporated when her eye caught the gleam of the metal box and her heart gave a little jump. It might all be pointless, but pointless in style. No point dwelling on sad thoughts, not when there was money to be spent.

The fog turned orange, an explosion, muffled but deep, followed by the high-pitched whistle of a ship's alarm.

Clarissa lifted the flag and waved it in triumph. The Pensioner Pirates of Marine Parade had struck again and she laughed at the fog, gave the metal box a loving stroke and blew Daphne a last fond kiss.

Jonathan Broughton:

Dark Reunion: Twenty Short Stories includes all of my short stories. They include tales of the paranormal, of horror, a little humour and some that are poignant.

Running Before the Midnight Bell is an urban thriller set in Hastings and St Leonards on Sea, UK. Detective Inspector Anthony Nemo hunts for a killer, a killer who threatens to expose his own vulnerabilities.

I wrote *The Russian White* when I still lived in London. Based on the visit of the Russian Tsar, Peter the Great, when he visited Britain at the end of the 17th century and gave, as a gift to King William the Third, a huge uncut diamond. This diamond was lost and I invented a tale, set in Victorian London at the outbreak of the Crimean War, as to why it was lost and the efforts of Russian spies to find it and bring it back to Russia.My Author Page: amazon.com/author/jonathanbroughton

On Twitter: @jb121jonathan

On Facebook: facebook.com/jonathan.broughton.5

Aging is hard, but what are the alternatives?

Exile
By April Grey

"St. Tropez is best in the off-season, don't you agree?"

My new acquaintance sat in the shade of the palm tree and sipped her tall, perspiring drink. I was wondering how long I should stay. Would it be intolerably rude to just get up and walk away after her one sentence? And did it matter?

I smiled and pushed up my sunglasses to the top of my head. A fellow American here on the Cote D'Azur and staying at the same very exclusive spa as myself, didn't she merit a morsel of kindness? Her hair was dyed, as was mine, to hold back the burgeoning grey, and she'd also done all the necessary nipping and tucking so common among women of our station. I had avoided the knife; was as "God made me," except for the hair dye.

Still, I preferred not to look in mirrors nowadays—the hard and lean woman with emerald chips for eyes who stared back at me was an evil disillusionment to my ego. I suppose when it got intolerable I, too, would chase the elusive dream of youth with Botox and the scalpel.

I held out my hand, choosing on whim to be sociable. "My name is Madeleine Jameson, and I do prefer my resorts to be out-of-season."

She happily beamed at me. Oh, yes, now we would be friends for all eternity. I could see that as she took my hand in both of hers.

"I'm Ricki Shannon." Oozing with bonhomie, she hailed our poolside waiter, and ordered a second round of drinks for us both.

I gazed up at the perfect blue sky and calculated that it had to be about four p.m. and way too early to be on my second drink. Still I sat back and relished my Gimlet. It was sweet and tart, you could tell they prepared it with fresh limes, and it was all that I ever wanted from a cocktail.

And a cocktail was about all I required from my life.

Ricki sallied forth with the requisite tales of the trials and tribulations of the fabulously wealthy; her children, her divorce, and her subsequent affairs now that her kids were too old to need her or care if she was around. They had their trust funds and lacked for nothing. She sat back and waited for my story. I gave the short, sweet version; married late, no kids, and widowed—no affairs. The look on her face was at first incredulous and then pitying.

I should have left as soon as she sat down.

"But my dear, don't you get," she paused for emphasis, "lonely?"

I stretched out my too long legs, legs that had paid the rent in better days, and had taken care of me for over thirty years before their betrayal. "I'm used to being alone."

Her voice lowered as if she were about to discuss a state secret. "Don't you ever miss being in someone's arms?"

I wasn't sure where this was leading to. Was she bi? I'd known women like that in the chorus at Vegas, and they weren't my cup of tea. No one was—except Gilbert, and only because his lawyer had written up an amazingly, iron-clad pre-nup which not a single relative of his could hope to ever compromise. It was Kismet, our meeting at the rehab center after my tendon had snapped. At my age, my career—already much longer than most—would be completely over by the time my injury healed and my bank account would have been drained.

Gilbert was learning how to walk on the aluminum leg they gave him after the cancer had taken his real one. On his deathbed he confessed he'd lied to me about being in remission. He told me that he just wanted to die looking at something beautiful. I was a model wife straight through the funeral, and then I left it all behind.

But my bosom companion here didn't need to know about my plebian past. My life was quite comfortable and after the second drink, pleasingly numb. The sun sank a bit lower, cutting below the shade of the tree and striking me, blinding me. I shifted my chair. In that moment I thought about my mother; what would she have thought if she were still alive? She'd worked hard, slinging hash, right up until the day she died of a stroke while having her cigarette break behind Pete's Diner where she worked. I could almost hear her saying "a woman's got to keep her wits about her." Sure mom, that's why I stop at two drinks.

"Well, let me tell you," she continued in the same breathy undertone, "I have found a treasure."

I put the glasses back on. I had been polite. I had shared a little. Now it was time for her to either go away or shut up.

"His name is Cesar. And what a honey he is."

Okay, I was curious. "A masseur?" I asked, peering over my glasses at her. I had to admit I was in need of a good rub down and my leg, in spite of all the daily swimming, sorely missed therapeutic touch. It gave a little warning twinge as if to remind me how badly I'd been neglecting it.

"A paramour, a gigolo." She giggled girlishly, and it wasn't very becoming.

I stiffened and held on to my resolution to be nice, though I wasn't sure why. "Surely, a women as lovely and well-maintained as yourself shouldn't have to—" I managed to say with straight face.

"Darling, at our ages, the only thing a handsome man wants from us is our money. It is much, much better to pay upfront—less heartache." She gestured to the poolside attendant and he immediately came over to refresh our drinks. I had a feeling she didn't bother with two drink limits.

"Well thank you for the advice." I got up and dove into the pool, knowing I'd fulfilled my quota of being hospitable for the week. Again, I really couldn't say why I made the pretense of being interested in the humdrum affairs of the rich and bored, being one of them made them no less dull than when I'd been on the other side of the stage lights in Vegas. When I returned to get my towel, to my relief she'd left.

A day went by, blending into all the other days and weeks of sun and water, expensive meals and drinks by the poolside. Ricki and her stupid suggestion were forgotten. Not that I had much on my mind—I didn't, and that was just the way I liked it. I had achieved a perfect Zen-like balance in my life, no ups and no downs, just this huge gaping emptiness in which I was immersed.

I was getting ready for bed when there was a knock on my door. I was surprised that security could be so lax. That wasn't what I was forking over the big bucks for. I put on my silk robe.

"Qui est la?" My French wasn't great, but flash enough Euros and you'd be surprised how many people knew English.

"Allo? Your friend, Ricki, she tells me…that…May I come in and speak to you?"

It took me a moment to remember who Ricki was. That lady by the side of the pool with her friend for hire. Right. And this would be her friend.

"Go away," I said through the door.

I heard a long string of French in a tone of voice indicating it wasn't Bible verses he was reciting.

"If you did not wish my services, why did you not say so to your friend?"

This was getting embarrassing. Half the hotel would know that I had ordered up a lover for myself. I opened the door a crack, and saw one of the most amazing men I ever had the pleasure of meeting. This is from Ms. Jaded, someone who had worked in Vegas her entire life and had seen every pretty boy and bad boy and in between. It wasn't his looks, no they were quite average, but something electrified me in his presence. This was charisma on steroids and all I could do was stand there and gape.

"Have you changed your mind? Am I invited in?" His accent was charming, and did I mention that I'm not easily charmed? I nodded. The hallway was filled with this golden glow. And I was glowing right along with it.

Black, longish hair, pale skin and brown eyes with a lean, sleek physique; I couldn't stop myself from staring into his eyes. This sort of beauty wasn't meant for humans.

I was in the presence of the sublime.

"May I come in?"

His faltering English roused me from my stupor. I nodded and stepped aside. Catching my breath I realized that I had just invited a total stranger into my suite and I wasn't dressed. I shook my head trying to clear it. At first he had seemed quite young, but now older, no, ageless. His movements were as graceful as any dancer I had ever met.

What was going on with me?

A woman in her mature years doesn't start acting like a giggling teen at her first dance, except this mature woman was.

"Why—" I couldn't even form the question, didn't know which words to use.

"Why am I here?" He flashed a smile revealing deep laugh lines on the sides of his face. "I ask myself the same. A young, beautiful woman such as yourself obviously has no need of my services. I should have left immediately but you have enthralled—"

The over-rehearsed lines were a pail of cold water. "Oh, cut the crap. Do women really buy that line? You are a real gigolo?"

He looked to the ground and headed for the door. "Je m'excuse."

Yes, he should leave...but no, I couldn't. "How much?" I reached for my bag.

"My payment? Five hundred Euros. You can leave the money tomorrow at the front desk."

I wanted to say no, the amount was too high, but

panic welled up in me at the thought of letting him go. I couldn't do it. "Deal. Umm, d'accord!"

"And there is one more thing."

I was ready to leap through hoops of fire to get at him. But then he produced from his jacket pocket a pair of dentures, the incisors of which were overlarge and seemed rather pointy.

"A little bit of role playing." He smiled.

"Blood play?" I wasn't born yesterday and as they say what happens in Vegas stays in Vegas. I had seen it all.

"You will feel nothing more than a prick, and no scars will be left. I swear to you there will be no harm."

"Yeah, until I find out I've got AIDS or Hepatitis…"

"On my word as a gentleman."

It was stupid, dangerous.

But again, the word "no" wouldn't come.

He slipped out of his black, light-weight jacket and I could see his muscles ripple under the linen of his dark blue shirt.

I felt a tremor go through me and a bead of perspiration stung my eyes.

I hadn't been this scared or aroused when I lost my virginity, nor on my wedding night.

Though I've always been a cool customer when it came to relationships, yet here I felt incredibly fragile, like a china doll about to be launched into the air.

And I was paying how much for this?

He placed the jacket on the back of my armchair and loosened his tie. Giving me a quick, winning smile he shoved the fake teeth into his mouth.

But he hadn't. He had palmed them and slipped them into his pants pocket!

A showgirl gets to see a lot of magic acts. I'd seen all the greats and this guy wasn't one of them. There's big magic, like making a 747 disappear and then there is sleight of hand which takes rapid reflexes and the ability to distract. He was fast, but he hadn't distracted me enough. And a new fear took hold as I wondered what his game was. Still, I felt paralyzed as much by terror as by lust. What was he playing at? He continued to remove his clothes as I stood frozen to the spot.

He smiled again, revealing impossibly sharp fangs. I wanted to scream but I couldn't. I shivered but it was from a dull heat that was traveling up from my sex. I had never been so aroused in my life.

Being out of control was a new sensation. The fear kept swirling around mixing with lust, making my arousal ever more intense. I wanted him…I wanted to feel his mouth on my neck, my breasts, and on my tender, most intimate place. And I wanted to feel his bite. He removed the last of his clothing and my eyes took in his glorious alabaster form for a few seconds before he moved closer to me. His fingers were cool on my inflamed skin. My robe slipped down over my shoulders and onto the floor. We were naked together. He caressed my breasts and I entered a fever dream with his water-cool touch sliding over my burning skin. He had me on my back and then he was kissing my breasts while his hand glided lower to where I was hot and swollen. It was hard to follow what was going on, overwhelmed as I was by the ache in my groin, and then the cool relief of him slipping into me.

His movements as he pleasured me were slow and careful. And then my muscles clenched and I thrust upwards against him. I felt his mouth on my neck, sucking and swallowing as my body continued to convulse.

Someone was screaming and I wondered idly if it were me.

I felt him stir and then the weight shifted on the bed. Stretching out my arm, I held onto him.

"Why?" I asked.

He looked confused.

"You don't need to sell yourself. You are a vampire."

"And what does that mean?" He raised his eyebrows, looking philosophical. "How many people are paid to eat their dinner?"

"But—"

"Since you have seen through my little rouse, I will tell you. The stories written of my kind portraying us as rich royalty, they are all stupid."

"I'm sorry, I didn't mean to prejudge. Hell, you aren't even supposed to exist."

His eyes flashed. "And we prefer it that way. Anyone too obvious is removed for the good of the rest."

"Well, thanks for the information." I felt incredibly gauche for offending him. I could have shown more tact. After all how many people assumed that I had been a showgirl because I was too dumb to be anything else. Heck, I could have gotten a college scholarship, but there was no need. I loved the stage, the excitement, the crazy getups I wore, but most of all the dancing. The money for those dance classes when I was a girl wasn't easily come by but they paid off.

"You are one of the most beautiful women I've had the pleasure to be with."

I blushed. This time my bullshit detector didn't go off.

"I should like to make a proposition."

"Yes?"

"My kind stay isolated and do not, as the movies show, live together in castles and basements like a flock of bats. And I am never with a woman more than once. To have a relationship would lead to her being converted to what I am. Eternal life is also eternal night. Not many enjoy it."

I impulsively squeezed his hand. It was pretty obvious from the sadness in his eyes that he didn't enjoy his life, or lack of it.

To my surprise he returned the pressure. "I would like to see you again. It has been too long since I have been able to speak openly to anyone. Please do not give me your answer right away. Leave a message downstairs at the desk for me."

The next day I left the money, and a message that I would like to see him. All day I was in a state of heightened excitement. I was more alive than I'd been in years. I felt dizzy with the thought of seeing him again. Sad. Pathetic, I know, but I had fallen in love for the first time in my life. If he wanted me, well, I was his, having taken the bait: hook, line and sinker.

Just after nightfall, I sat in my room, waiting. I had had my hair color touched up. It was a dark titian red which closely matched my original hair color. And I wore a new dress made of watery green silk. I felt ready to go to the prom. When the phone rang, I nearly jumped out of my skin.

"Come meet me at Boulevard Café, down by the harbor."

He sat in a dark corner of the sidewalk cafe, nursing or pretending to nurse a double espresso and watching the lights of the boats going by. He wore a black leather jacket and a white shirt. He was as exquisite as I remembered, more so.

After ordering a Campari, I told him a little of my life. Then it was his turn.

"My father owned a bakery and our family, my sisters and me, lived in an apartment over it. He'd be up early every morning, slapping the bread, forcing life into it. That bakery was his kingdom and I was the crown prince. There was never any question of my not taking over the family business.

But then the Germans came, and my father took ill, too sick to leave his bed. I wanted to go fight, but the family needed me. Still, I would sneak away to spend time with the men who eventually would form the Maquis, the resistance.

"Then the dirty Nazi pigs came sniffing after my sisters. I caught one bringing my youngest sister home after a "date." With the knife I used for loaves of bread, I slashed open his face. I should have killed him, but the scar would remind him of his evil to his last days. Of course, I could not stay after that, so I ran and joined the Maquis. Weeks later, I got word of my father's death. I still wonder if it was from a broken heart." He hunched over his coffee, seeming to shrink into his self as the memories took over.

"One of the members of my resistance group was a Gypsy. He was half crazed, his whole family sent to the camps, and he would talk about this place, not far into Austria where the Gypsies knew of a very evil man. The man had powers, amazing powers of life and death. And maybe if we went there he could help us win out over the bastards who had occupied our country.

"Five of us snuck over the border into Switzerland and then Austria. We found the place. A filthy half acre of a junk yard inhabited by a fat little man and a dozen mongrel dogs.

One of our group panicked when he realized what he would become and tried to leave. The dogs ripped out his throat. The rest of us stayed and allowed ourselves to be used and then changed. The little man was like a tick, swelling huge on our blood."

He covered his eyes with his hand. My heart leapt in sympathy but I left him to his feelings. Minutes went by and then he continued.

"We had our revenge on the Germans. We bathed in their blood, feasting on anyone who wore their uniform. We did not stay together long. Seeing one another was like looking into a mirror and none of us could stand what we saw. The blood lust was so strong and though we started with a noble purpose, every death seemed to degrade us further, damning us. We killed and killed again, and then the war ended, but not for us. We still craved blood."

The agony in his eyes proved that he was more human than he'd ever believe. He pulled out a cigarette from his jacket and lit it with shaking hands. I didn't know he smoked. I hadn't tasted it on his lips.

"I had four sisters. After more than six decades, only two remain; one senile and the other blind. But back then after the war I couldn't go back to my family or my old life. I was so changed—they would know.

"I paid a lawyer to keep check on them. I had reports every six months, who got married, who had a baby and pictures as well. I set up a trust for them so if anyone in my family needed something, a special operation or something extra for school, they would have it. I am now a great granduncle and I know the names of every child and adult, what they like to do and where they go to school or work.

"I live through them and for them. They are still my family."

"That's why you charge women?" Those kids probably had diamond-encrusted running shoes at this point.

"They are my only connection left with life, although they are only names and faces in photographs."

"They don't know who you are—you could go visit them. Claim you're a long lost cousin."

He shook his head and inhaled deeply before slowly releasing a blue cloud of smoke.

What was I to say, I'm sorry? I didn't have any family at all. He had more going for him than I did.

We were both silent a little while, thinking our own thoughts and then I said, "Tell me, do you dance?"

He shrugged his shoulders. "As you Americans say, two left feet."

"That's a shame. You carry yourself well."

We walked slowly back to my room. This time the sex was on the house. He was more relaxed, less professional, at times playful, and then needy in his lovemaking. Just being himself, I guess. But for me, the climaxes meant nothing because all I could think about, like some junkie, was when he'd sink his teeth into me. I craved it; I wanted him to suck me dry. Of course, he didn't do that. If he did it then, I'd die and not be turned. Some sort of a third date rule.

When dawn was nearing and he'd quenched himself, he kissed and nuzzled me all over, whispering endearments in French, saying that he loved me. He promised that that night we'd be united forever. My aging process would stop, and my leg would be as good as new. I'd be able to dance again.

After he left, I got dressed and headed out. I watched the sunrise glinting on the harbor, and breathed in the brisk, early morning air.

I hadn't known the options before: there had been just life or the yawning grave.

I knew an actor who, when he was in his cups, used to quote his favorite playwright. He said once, "They give birth astride of a grave, the light gleams an instant, then it's night once more." I admit he was only entertaining when he was drunk. The rest of the time he was an arrogant prick. I hadn't thought of him in over twenty years.

Cesar was the living dead: we had that much in common. I thought about eternity with him as I returned to my room.

And then I packed my bags.

Vegas hadn't changed. New places mushroomed up every day while other places went bust. But it's home.

I bought a small dance studio and set up a school.

At first my leg hurt like a bitch at the end of a day of teaching, but I paid for the best damned physical therapy money could buy and I had a flare for teaching that made it all worthwhile. Best of all, since money is never an issue, the ones who are really talented and can't afford to pay, I give them scholarships. It feels good to be a foster mom to all those aspiring dancers.

A few weeks ago, I ran into this guy I knew from back when I was in the chorus. Jack's about ten years younger than me, tanned, blond with blue eyes. He dances in the big extravaganza over at Bally's, but he knows he can't compete much longer with the younger men coming in. His looks are going and he worries that he's getting man tits. I told him it didn't bother me, but he could get a boob job if he thought it would make a difference.

On his nights off from work we go out dancing together and then we wind up making love. He wants to marry me. I don't know if it will last—but who cares? You gotta dance while you can.

Sometimes I wake up in the middle of the night and I feel this old ache, a yearning to be taken, but immortality brings its own pain, so I remind myself that he was just a gigolo.

April Grey's short stories, published in both print anthologies and on-line, are collected in *The Fairy Cake Bakeshop* and in *I'll Love You Forever*. She edited the anthology *Hell's Garden: Mad, Bad and Ghostly Gardeners*. Her urban fantasy novels *Chasing the Trickster* and *St. Nick's Favor* are available at her author page.

Her dark fantasy novel, *Finding Perdita* will be published by Caliburn Press next year.

aprilgrey.blogspot.com

Hell's Grannies

author.to/aprilgrey
aprilgrey.com
twitter @aprilgreynyc
facebook.com/april.grey.5

In Australia Julia Mason discovers ancient forces are at work.

Watchers of Old
By Judith Rook

"Grandma?"

Looking up from the vegetables, Julia Mason found her granddaughter's eyes fixed on her with thoughtful concentration.

"Yes, Poppy?" She smiled at the eleven-year-old and continued to chop. This after-school hour was sacrosanct to the affairs of childhood. Poppy could do whatever she wanted to do; no chores were allowed to intrude.

"Jackson Bird had another bruise today. He said it hurt."

The knife stopped for a moment. "Did he, pet? Where was it?"

"On the top of his arm, like last time. Right on the top. He showed it to me. He said his dad punched him again."

"That must hurt. Was he upset?"

"I don't know. He said it was OK but he looked down a lot. You know, more than he does usually, and he wouldn't put his hand up in maths. And he said I mustn't tell anyone because it would upset his mum. I didn't promise. I wanted to tell you and Dad but I won't tell anyone else."

45

"Best not to, pet. People have got to keep things private, although sometimes not too private. Friends can always help."

"It's funny. Jackson's dad is a really nice man. Why would he hit him so hard? When he brings Jackson to school he always says hello to Mrs Leonetti and makes her laugh."

"I don't know, pet. Sometimes adults have a lot of things to cope with."

Poppy slid off the tall stool. "Will you tell Dad?"

"I will, duck. Now where are you off to?"

"My cubby house . . . Grandma?"

"Yes, Poppy?"

"Do you think you and Mrs Morrison and the other ladies could do something?"

Julia stopped chopping and opened the door to the backyard. "Off you go. It'll be homework time before you know it."

"Yes, but will you ask them?"

"I'll probably have coffee tomorrow morning at the home. Will that do?"

"Yes, great! Thank you, Grandma. Will you say 'hello' to Mrs Morrison for me?" The girl skipped off.

Julia stared after her for a moment. She had almost decided not to visit the home tomorrow. They hadn't rung. Julia had been given nothing to do, and the last time she saw the ladies, Adeline Morrison had been even more remote than usual, going back to her room after only a few minutes.

"She's busy," said one of the ladies. "Cutting," said the other. "It goes on all the time, of course but when she's with us, you don't notice it. She'll be back with us soon because something is going to happen; something's coming close. Atr . . . Adeline can't do everything from a distance all of the time; and it's laid down that every so often we have to be with people.

Laid down? Be with people? Julia added to her collection of uncomfortable thoughts about the old ladies.

After tea, stacking the dishwasher, Julia asked David, her divorced son, about Jackson Bird's father.

"Ken Bird? Well, I know who he is. Nice bloke. He's a Fly-in Fly-out worker – flies up to Newman, seven days on, seven days off, and when he's around he goes down to the town's social club a lot. Why are you asking about Ken Bird?"

"He punched his lad, the one in Poppy's class. She said he had a big bruise."

"Did he? Well, the boy probably . . . No, no! I'm sorry, Mum." The man put up his hands. "That came out wrong. No, Ken did the wrong thing, but you never know what's behind a punch, especially with a FIFO worker." He set the dishwasher going.

"Poppy?" he called.

"Up here, Dad!" Poppy was in her bedroom.

"I'm watching the news now. Then I want to see your homework."

"Yes, Dad. I've finished it."

"It can be bad, working up there," David turned to his mother again, "and it's the rainy season. He could have been stuck at the mine-site runway for hours, waiting for the water to clear; perhaps they had to fill in potholes before the plane could take off. And isn't he a haul truck driver? I can't see how anyone could ever feel safe driving one of those monsters!

Not surprising that he could have hit his kid without meaning to."

"Maybe, but the boy's such a skinny little thing."

"His mum seems to look after him well," offered her son, making for the lounge. "She's a good mother by all accounts. Ken's a good bloke."

And there you are, thought Julia. Jackson Bird is the son of a father under stress from work, if not for other reasons. If he punches his son, about four times smaller than him, it can be understood if not completely excused, and the man's still a good bloke.

This flying up to the north to work, nearly a thousand miles away from home, for the sake of the good money it brought in, had real problems attached. Seeing your children's faces on a screen as you said goodnight to them would get to a man, not to mention what might be happening in his wife's life and him not around to help her or detect the signs. Yes, the money was good, but a family might end up paying too highly in other currency for it. Well, she decided, tomorrow she'd take the matter further. She'd talk to the old ladies.

She thought about Poppy and her friend, Mrs Morrison. About a year ago the three ladies, Julia's employers, had been at a table outside Moxi's Café in the main street of the small town. They called Julia across because there was something she needed to hear, and Poppy came too.

"Leave your lassie with me," Adeline Morrison said. "You talk to Evelyn and Dot."

While Julia spoke to the two other ladies as instructed, Poppy and the old woman talked to each other, Adeline patting the girl's hand now and then.

Sitting back at the end the old lady nodded. "You and I will do fine, my honey. Make sure that your grandma brings you here again."

Some months later Mrs Morrison presented Poppy with a crystal ball, bigger than a tennis ball but still small enough to be held in the palm of an adult hand. It was a true crystal, made of polished quartz and not of glass.

"This is great," said the girl on their return home. "Look, Grandma, you can see into it but you can't always see through it. Mrs Morrison said that I should put it away until I'm a woman, so I'll need a box."

From her store of this and that Julia found a box that would do. It was made of wood, had a hinged top with a latch and was decorated with painted roses and lavender. Poppy carefully wrapped the crystal ball in tissue paper and placed it in the box.

"When I'm grown up," she said, giving it to her grandmother. With a slight shiver, a glimpse into an impossible future, Julia placed the box on the top shelf of the hall closet. "You remember where it is," she told her granddaughter. It would probably be best if she herself did not touch the crystal ball again.

In the first year of her retirement Julia went with a choir one day to sing at an old people's home and met Evelyn Ward. Some ten years older than Julia, Evelyn was a brisk little body, with silver hair cut quite short. At the post-concert tea, seeing the other woman's arthritic hands as she fumbled with her cup, Julia placed a scone on her neighbour's plate.

"You might as well cut it for me, while you're at it."

Despite her age, the woman's voice was strong.

"I'm Evelyn Ward. Been here five years and like it well enough. But it's not what you expect, is it? Not when you're in your forties and going to operas and concerts and dinner parties."

"Well, no . . ." Julia felt her way cautiously.

"You must be retired, otherwise you wouldn't be singing here in the middle of the afternoon."

"I could have taken time off."

"Well, did you?"

Julia laughed. "You've got me. No, I didn't. I'm retired, but I'm still settling into the change. Things are very different."

She caught a sharp glance from the older woman. "It happens to us all."

At the next choir rehearsal, Julia was handed a note from Mrs E Ward inviting her to morning coffee at the home "with friends". It was a formal, old-fashioned communication, and Julia accepted with a short letter sent through the post.

The "friends" were two ladies of about Evelyn's age, one named Dot Hunter, pleasant and sociable, with pepper and salt hair scrambled into an untidy bun on top of her head. Then there was Mrs Adeline Morrison, dark of hair and eyebrows and noticeable for her large and prominent nose. She sat shrunken in upon herself, shawl around her shoulders, seemingly ignored by the others. Evelyn and Dot, however, were sharp as tacks and after the cups and plates had been put to the side Evelyn turned to Julia.

"We think there may be a job for you with us."

"A job?" Julia was taken aback.

The staff member who had brought their coffee reappeared, making for their group; but she paused, looked around the room with a puzzled expression and turned to another table.

"We don't move about as we used to," said Evelyn, "but we need to know what's going on. If you're cooped up here you can't get down to the town easily, except on the days the bus comes, and none of us drive much now. We had a lady, but she's moved to Queensland and we thought perhaps you might . . ."

"Do you want me to help you get to the shops? I'm not sure . . . I mean, I'd like to, but would I be able to do it? Would there be things like wheelchairs?"

"No, no! Nothing like that," said Dot. "What we need is someone to do some walking around for us, someone who can go and see things for us, perhaps even talk to people."

"But what about your families? Couldn't they . . . ?"

"Ah well, that's just the thing, you see." Evelyn took up the thread. "You know what families are like; busy . . . busy . . . And anyway, we don't want to bother them too much with our affairs. They begin to feel responsible, and then they begin to interfere. No, what we do with our own time is not for our families to know.

"It will just be a bit of going around the town, mainly. You could probably work it in with your own shopping trips, but you could find the things we need to see then come back and tell us."

"I don't understand . . ."

Mrs Morrison suddenly looked up at her with black eyes, rounds of polished coal. Her skin was smooth over sharp cheekbones but wrinkled around her mouth and chin.

"You give us a go, my honey." The voice was slightly hoarse, softly rattling in the back of the woman's throat.

"Do one trip for us, and then if you don't like it we'll go our ways and say nothing more."

There was something about her words, something about her voice but especially there was something about her eyes. Eyes that shone with a hard, compelling power, turning the woman's face into an expressionless mask where old age was not the dominant feature. Julia looked into those strange eyes and they drew her away, into a place where she saw the light she remembered from her girlhood. The wind she remembered was there as well; she felt the wind again, and she threw back her head and breathed deeply, rejoicing in the world she knew. But she wasn't on the wheat-belt farm; she was in Harmouth in an old people's home where she sat at a table with three elderly women peering at her.

Julia pulled herself together. Well, why not? These old dears couldn't want very much and if it made them happy . . . "All right, I'll do it; I've got the time. Do you have something particular in mind?"

"Could you get up early for a couple of days, dear, and go for a walk?" said Dot.

Across the room the waitress glanced in their direction, smiled, shook her head and began to approach them again.

It was the middle of summer. For three days Julia got up at half-past five and joined the early morning dog-walkers along the shoreline of the wide inlet where the town lay and which gave access to the great ocean leading to the far south.

The ladies had asked her to be around the town's yacht club and notice things that might be a little out of the ordinary. Julia did not need to go looking; noticing was forced on her. At six o'clock, some huge earth-moving machines, preparing the ground for a large luxury housing development, began their infernal beep-beeping, and growling. What a dreadful start to the day for the people living in the houses nearby! Weren't there by-laws limiting the beginning time of such noises?

She had coffee again in the aged care home. She told the ladies about the noisy mornings around the yacht club and they smiled at each other, except for Mrs Morrison who looked down into her lap where her hands were working on something that could not be seen.

"Right, Dot. Over to you." Bun wobbling dangerously, Dot scrabbled inside a very large purple handbag, bringing out a small notebook with a smiley face on the front. "Six o'clock? Thank you dear."

"Dot's friend's grandson knows the brother of one of the site foremen," said Evelyn."

"Mum?" said David, a few days later, "did you see anything about this when you went on those morning walks?" He waved the local community weekend newspaper at her. On the front page there was a scoop telling of an informal strike at the construction site near the yacht club.

"The drivers won't begin now before half-past seven. Something's scared them. On Tuesday they couldn't open the gates into the site. They had to cut a hole in the cyclone fence and when they got in they found that the machines had been moved during the night; they'd been put in a circle, and apparently they were hard to start. The police can't find evidence of sabotage, but someone's told the blokes that if they begin work at half-past seven, there will be no problem. You were out early exactly when this was happening. Did you see anything? And now I come to think of it, why have you stopped the walks?"

"I saw nothing," said Julia truthfully, "and actually it was a bit too early for me."

There was turmoil in Harmouth over the matter. Labour unions became involved because there was obviously a safety issue somewhere, and the story was taken up by the big city papers. Finally the developer of the site had to capitulate and the drivers began to start work at half-past seven in accordance with the Council by-laws. The local population was gleeful. It was felt that this particular developer, an arrogant bastard by all accounts, had got his comeuppance, although no one really understood what had happened.

Julia had an inkling. "Dot's friend's grandson knows the brother of one of the site foremen," Evelyn had said. But what about the gates and the machines that moved in the night?

That had been about a year ago and now Julia was well established as the roving member of the group, the gofer who claimed expenses, who went around gathering information and other things for the older women, sometimes arranging that certain people should appear in the town's main street on days when three old dears from the care home had their morning coffee and cakes outside Moxi's Café.

"Sometimes we just have to see people," said Evelyn. "You can only go so far with knowing things. It often comes to the point when Atrop . . . Adeline . . . well, when we really need to see what they look like."

Julia's politeness taught her not to ask questions, but in the first weeks she felt something about Mrs

Morrison that disturbed her. Sometimes she sensed an amused remoteness, as though the old woman knew too much, as though she found ordinary life unimportant. Sometimes she looked at Julia out of her black eyes with an unmoving, appraising look, and Julia had to fight to keep hidden the things about her life that she desperately wanted to tell Mrs Adeline Morrison.

The doubt nagged at her, and the feeling that she should make a break built up until, about six months after the first meeting, Julia went to the home to tell the ladies that she would withdraw from the group. Only Mrs Morrison was to be found in her small apartment, and for the first time Julia was alone with the shrivelled old woman. Later, she remembered nothing specific about what had happened in the room, but when she got home she had an impression that she had been pulled away from something dangerous and she felt happy, optimistic, full of the joy of life – and at her age!

Julia kept on with her work for the group, finding herself briefly involved with people from all parts of the town. For example, there was a man who helped to coach a local football team – the colts, the young up and coming players. One Wednesday morning he gave a pleasant greeting to the old ladies as he walked past them on the way to his office, and Adeline Morrison stared after him, while Evelyn casually pushed a pebble around on the surface of the table. Not very long after, Julia learned the football club needed another assistant coach. She nodded at this. There was a rumour that the man might be one who got out of bed on the wrong side.

Two weeks before Poppy told her about Jackson Bird, Julia drove Evelyn and Dot out of town to a waterhole hidden within a large belt of bush, and reached along a rough unsealed road. All around was quiet and still. Above the tree line the sky was darkening with the distant approach of a summer storm. On the far side of the pool a large outcrop of rock could be seen, rising perhaps fifteen metres above the water.

"It's over there," said Evelyn, pointing across. "We need more of these." She showed Julia a small water-rounded pebble, about the size of a toffee. It was dark in colour with veins of a lighter mineral running through it.

"As many as you can, dear. And the colours have to be there."

Her employers gave her the strangest things to do, thought Julia, cautiously picking her way towards the other side of the pool. She needed to be careful because the ground sloped quite steeply towards the water and there was no path. Few people came here; that was for sure, and she wished the air beneath the ancient jarrah and karri was not quite so still. There was something around. She stopped, alarmed, peering through the bare trunks of the quiet, tall trees. She felt as though there was an invisible barrier around her, keeping out sound. Behind her, when she looked, Dot and Evelyn were outlined against the lowering sky and Julia felt easier.

But then she almost slid away into the place where human minds go when the borders of reality are broken. Around the familiar figures, obscuring them, overlaying them, she perceived larger shapes, diaphanous, luminous against the distant storm clouds, with soft, full

56

garments moving in a non-existent wind, half-draped over elaborately dressed hair.

In the onset of terror; heart pounding dangerously, lungs clawing for air, Julia stared at the apparitions. Hands pressed against her chest she took one unsteady step backwards. The faces, blank-eyed and ageless, smiling with cosmic inhuman amusement turned towards her. One of the figures raised an arm, pointing upwards; the other held wide-spread hands as though it might be assessing the length of something unseen. Both figures began to laugh but there was no sound. The pointing finger moved directly to Julia.

"No!" Julia stumbled backwards again. She closed her eyes against the mask-like faces, faces lacking all human expression. "No! What are you? Evelyn . . . ? Dot . . . ? She half fell against a low bush. Turning to look at something beyond Julia's sight the unearthly figures began to fade.

She made it to a partly buried fallen tree and sat on it with her face in her hands. Her whole body was shaking. She had just seen something that no one should have seen. There was no such thing as what she had just seen. Whatever it had been, it did not exist. It was not part of the world of ordinary reality.

She would go back immediately, tell the ladies she had forgotten an appointment, take them home and never see them or Adeline Morrison again! Hands, measuring? Her memory supplied a thought. Three Fates, figures from the world's ancient stories; one of them measured the span of a person's life. She sat on the log, trembling and nauseous.

"Julia? What are you doing?" It was Evelyn's voice. She had been the pointer, the one who span the thread of mortal life.

"Are you all right, dear?" Dot was more caring, more concerned. The one who measured the time allotted to a life also helped to form its course.

Unable to answer, Julia's mind struggled, desperate to avoid acceptance of the unacceptable.

"She's not well. Look, Evelyn. Julia's had a bad turn. I can get through those bushes, I think. You get your mobile ready while I go and have a look at her."

"No, no! Stay there! I'm all right." Something rose in Julia and she got unsteadily to her feet. What she had seen might have existed; or it might have come out of her own mind. But she had not been hurt. Only her beliefs had been disturbed, and beliefs could be put to one side for future consideration. "I'm fine. I just felt dizzy for a moment. The air's pretty thick in here. I'll go on in a moment."

And go on she did. She reached the other side of the waterhole and the rock outcrop. Behind it she found smooth pebbles with streaks of different minerals running through them and collected about thirty. But geologically, these stones should not have been where they were. Again she felt the presence of a watcher. The silence was almost complete and the scents of the bush were as strong as she had ever smelled them.

Turning to leave, she caught sight of a movement. Half-hidden by the thick undergrowth, stood an aboriginal woman dressed in a simple but colourfully patterned frock. Speechless, Julia stared, until with a smile the younger woman faded away into the bush.

"Look how many she's found!" said Evelyn in delight. "It likes you, Julia, that's certain."

"What likes me? There was someone watching me; a young woman, a Noongar woman." Julia used the name of the tribe which had cared for this part of the great continent for over forty thousand years.

Evelyn and Dot smiled at each other. "Well, perhaps, but it's just the bush. Nothing to worry about. Nothing will ever bother you when you're with us."

Now Julia told the three older ladies about Ken Bird. "I have the feeling that he's a troubled man," she said. Mrs Morrison lifted her head. Her brightly black eyes, glittered in a way that Julia had seen before but had never been able to explain with any degree of satisfaction to herself. She only knew that the gaze, apparently coming from a distance, meant that Mrs Morrison was particularly interested.

"He wants money, is that it?"

"He earns a lot but he could still need more. I don't know. Shall I try to find out?"

Armed with the approval of the three old ladies, within two weeks Julia discovered that Ken Bird had a gambling problem. It wasn't difficult. She enlisted the help of a friend whose daughter worked in the town's social club. Over three days, during one of the man's periods at home, the young woman kept a casual notice of his appearances.

"He comes and goes," said Julia's friend. "He'll be in for an hour with his dad, then he'll leave but he'll come back for lunch. Then, after lunch he'll leave again. Apparently he's a nice sort of bloke but Ella thinks he bets on the horses; he carries the form guide around. Well, he must have plenty of money to gamble with, but it's a fool's game."

Just to make sure, Julia asked David, who enjoyed a little flutter, if he ever noticed Mr Bird in the betting shop.

"He goes in," said David. "Mum, will you stop this poking around in other people's affairs? It's going to get you noticed, and people don't like it."

But Julia persisted. She walked past the Bird house a couple of times until she saw the wife out in the garden. When she stopped to admire the roses over the fence the woman spoke to her from a strained face and inward-looking eyes. Sure signs that all was not well.

"This one needs to come close," said Mrs Morrison. "We'll draw him."

Two Saturday mornings later Julia joined the older women outside Moxi's Café. Poppy was with her and after a strawberry milk shake the girl stood at the edge of the cluster of tables, watching the passers-by with interest. "Grandma! It's Jackson!" Poppy waved vigorously across to the other side of the street.

Julia looked at the old ladies. Evelyn placed a finger over her lips took something from her handbag, placing it on the table. It was one of the small stones Julia had found around the waterhole.

"He's coming across, Grandma. His dad's with him." Poppy retreated to stand by Julia. A man of good height with broad shoulders, probably in his late thirties, followed a boy of Poppy's age to the table.

"Hi, Poppy. Dad, it's Poppy; she's in Mrs Leonetti's class as well."

The man surveyed the group of elderly women without interest. "Mrs Mason. Nice to see you." He knew Julia from his son's school. "Sorry about this. Jackson wanted to come across but we'll have to be going. Always things to do on Saturday morning. Jackson, you can leave that." The boy and girl were already engrossed in a toy shop window nearby.

"Sit for a minute," said Mrs Morrison. Evelyn had begun to move the pebble aimlessly around the smooth top of the table. "Sit down for a moment and tell us about the work you do."

"Tell you about . . . ?" The man was astonished. "What do you want to know about my work? What has it got to do with you? Jackson . . . ?" But his eyes had been caught by the movement of Evelyn's hand and he took a chair.

"Julia," said Dot quietly. "Take the children for a while. We won't be long." This had happened before and Julia knew that while she was needed to arrange ways for the ladies to do whatever it was that they did, she was not to witness the actual operation.

Truth to tell, she did not want to see what happened. If she really got to know she might have to admit certain facts and look more closely into the "things in heaven and earth" that Shakespeare had talked about. She was not ready for that. She might never be ready, although perhaps Polly would be – one day.

She rose, collecting the boy and girl. They made for a well-known baker's shop further along the street where they queued to buy bread and cakes for tea. From a distance it appeared as though Jackson's father was merely having a conversation with three elderly ladies around an outside table.

"Where's Dad?" On the way out Jackson stopped, peering towards the café. "I can't see Dad! Mrs Mason, where's Dad? He's not there anymore! Where has he gone?" Julia also could not see Mr Bird. The whole table seemed to be covered by a mist, and people passing by skirted the edge without looking at it.

"Silly," Polly was amused. "He's there. He's just busy. He'll come back in a minute." Poppy easily accepted certain things that happened around the elderly ladies.

Before she had taken ten steps, Julia could see the man again quite clearly. He was restless, shifting in his chair, half-rising to his feet then sitting again, looking around. None of the passers-by paid any attention, but he caught sight of his son and waved to him impatiently.

"Oh, he's there! Jackson moved forward quickly.

Mrs Morrison said something and the man turned back to her, staring hard into her face.

As Julia and the two children reached the table she heard his words. ". . . bloody sticky-beaking old women. What gives you the right . . . ? You keep out of my affairs." He stood. "Jackson, move! We don't need to stay here any longer. And if I ever hear that you've been bandying my name about the town," he continued viciously, bending once again to Adeline Morrison placing a clenched hand before her on the table, "I'll see that you're stopped, old ladies or not."

From the side Evelyn's hand took his sleeve, pulling him slightly towards her. "Don't worry," she said. "We don't gossip. But you had to hear what has been said. What you do now is your own business."

He straightened. "I should make a complaint."

The women stared at him now with hard, remote faces, all evidence of grandmotherly empathy gone. In their unmoving eyes was the profound understanding of all the terrible, old wise women of the world. It was the inescapable knowledge of the Fates, the oldest of which, Atropos, cuts the thread of life; it was the aloof, impersonal power of the Norns and the deep, guiding wisdom of the female Australian ancients who knew the mysteries of their strange land, understanding its speech and what it required of the people who lived with it.

"The complaint has been heard." The oldest woman looked at the man until he dropped his eyes and his head and took his son away. Her hands were clasped. The small stone had disappeared.

"Mum," said David a week later at tea-time, "I heard something about Ken Bird today at work." Polly was immediately interested.

"What, Dad? What about Mr Bird?"

"He's coming home. Apparently he had an accident yesterday, up on the mine, and he probably won't work for months.

"Was he badly hurt?" Julia was interested too, and was that a pang of guilt that she felt? No, not guilt; relief, perhaps.

"Badly enough. His truck was taking on a two-hundred-and-fifty tonne payload of ore and there was a twenty-tonne boulder hidden in the smaller stuff. The driver of the big shovel didn't see the boulder when he picked the load up from the dig face, and he just dumped it into Ken's haul truck in the usual way. It seems that the impact was pretty violent. The truck didn't tip up, but Ken got thrown around badly. Seat restraints are never enough when that sort of thing happens and he was slammed into the side of the cab. Apparently he got a massive whiplash and broke his arm, but it could have been worse, far worse, and he can count himself lucky."

"What happened then, Dad?" Polly's eyes were wide.

"Oh, the usual," said David, smiling at his daughter. "The shovel driver saw what had happened and set off the accident signal three times: Emergency! Emergency! Emergency!" Polly's hands covered her mouth.

"When that happens on a mine-site, everything else on the airwaves closes down. Headquarters got the details in minutes and the helicopter picked him up before you could blink. You can ask your friend about it when you see him on Monday. His dad will be back by then and in the local hospital. What do you think? Shall I go to work on a mine-site?" He laughed and ruffled his daughter's hair.

"Dad!"

"Come on now, get your homework." Escaping from her father's reach, the girl went to the door, stuck her tongue out at him affectionately and went for her school bag.

"It might make a difference, though," David said as he left the table. "A bloke can get to thinking after something like that. Ken's bound to wonder about his family. What would happen to his wife and son if he wasn't around? He's a good bloke is Ken. A bit short-tempered, but a good bloke. At least he'll see more of his boy while he's off work, and who knows? Perhaps he'll forget the ponies for a while . . ." David paused at the door into the lounge room.

"I know what you're thinking, Mrs Mason. I don't know what you've actually been doing but I can read you like a book."

"Oh, I don't think so . . ." Julia laughed.

"Oh yes, I can; and I'm going to give you some advice. You and your old ladies should stop meddling in other people's affairs . . ." he paused and shook his head with resigned amusement at his mother . . . "although I don't suppose that's going to happen."

No, thought Julia, that's not going to happen.

By this time she had accepted that the three old women, while appearing in this world, belonged also to another place, another time; perhaps to other places and other times. What would be the point of discovering how they came to be living in Harmouth and what their true age was, if such things could be told? They would always find people like her, helpers, servers, and no person of small imagination would ever know the truth about them. Julia did not need to know this particular truth; she was content. She had a job now, and while she was the old ladies' assistant her life, if at times a bit weird, could only be useful and fulfilling. That was something she had no intention of changing.

"But I'll tell you one thing for the record," said her son. "Ken Bird was being looked after, up there on the mine. That accident could have permanently disabled him, even killed him. Easily!"

Judith Rook was raised in rural Yorkshire in the UK but now lives in Western Australia. After some years as a music journalist, Judith now writes novels as full-time as possible. She has written four science fiction books, with a fifth in preparation, and has also produced a fantasy romance. For reading, Sci-fi is Judith's favourite genre, followed by the great classics. She also has shelves of fantasy books. From time to time Judith stirs herself to rally around important social issues and has been known to take to the streets in protest, so long as there are good cafés along the way.

In her writing Judith periodically turns to short stories. She finds that the challenges of the genre strengthen the techniques which she uses in her novels.

Facebook: http://geni.us/JR1FB

Twitter: https://twitter.com/JudithRook2

Author Page : http://geni.us/JRpage

Sibling Rivalry can be fatal...

Fresh Finch
By Amy Grech

Doris Finch sat hunched in her rocking chair lost in the latest issue of *Prevention* when someone buzzed her apartment. "That must be Gerald. He's late as usual. Some people never change," she muttered to no one in particular.

She glanced at the framed picture of the twins on the mantel—Gerald and Simon—identical in every way: red hair, deep blue eyes, and stocky frames standing side by side on graduation day at NYU.

Doris adjusted her wire-rimmed spectacles carefully on the bridge of her nose and reached for the hickory crook resting on the windowsill beside her. Leaning on her cane, she got slowly to her feet and shuffled over to the intercom near the door and pressed the button that unlocked the lobby door without asking who her visitor was. Doris hardly ever had visitors.

Several minutes later, someone pounded on her door so hard it rattled. A quick peek through the peephole revealed the jagged face of her son, a tall man with thinning red hair. Doris fumbled with both deadbolts and the chain for a minute before she finally managed to open the door.

"Hello, Gerald. You're half an hour late, you know." She tapped her watch for emphasis. "I was beginning to wonder if you were going to show at all."

Simon flashed his winning smile, unsure how his brother would respond. "Sorry—traffic is murder this time of day—I rushed over from the East Side. Got here as fast as I could." He took her arm in his and started out the door. "Shall we?"

"Hold on, I can't find my keys! I don't want to get locked out!" Doris frowned and rearranged several piles of dog-eared magazines on the cluttered kitchen table. "Where did they go? I just had them. Honestly, I can't seem to find anything anymore."

"Calm down. Take a deep breath. Did you check your purse, Mother?" Simon rooted around in her bulky, leather bag and found them safely tucked away—easily forgotten—in one of the small compartments. "Here they are," he jingled them in the air, "where they can't possibly get lost. Can we go now?"

"I suppose so." Reluctantly, she gripped her cane tightly in her hand and leaned on her son's arm. They took the elevator down to the lobby and walked to Simon's nondescript black BMW parked at the curb.

"What happened to your navy blue Audi?" Doris stared at her son with inquisitive green eyes, magnified behind thick glasses.

Mother's keen observation caught him off guard. Simon suddenly remembered that Gerald was the more adventurous, successful one...."Oh, it's in the shop. Besides, I guessed it a bit too sporty for your tastes. You're always so buttoned-down." He sighed.

"Nonsense! This car reminds me of a hearse! Are you planning my funeral so soon?" With some difficulty, she sat down and buckled her seat belt.

"So now you think I expect you to die just because I happen to own a black car?! Really, Mother, I don't know where you get these crazy ideas!" Simon rolled his eyes.

Doris shrugged. "Never mind that! Let's get going before I miss the good bargains! You know how much I love a sale!"

He drove off. "Don't worry, Mother, you've got plenty of time to shop 'til you drop. I guarantee it."

She shifted in her seat; Doris clutched her purse in one hand and her cane in the other. "I want to believe you, but there are no guarantees."

"If you say so." Simon nodded absentmindedly as he wove through dense traffic with intense purpose. He headed towards Tiffany's on Fifth Avenue, where his dear, sweet mother frequently spent several hundred dollars during the course of her stay without thinking twice.

He stopped for a red light and leaned over to remove Mother's glasses before she could stop him.

"Gerald! What in the world are you doing? Now I can't see a thing!" Doris swatted blindly at the air as she struggled to get her bearings.

Simon tucked Mother's spectacles neatly into his shirt pocket and drove on. "Don't worry, Mother. Your glasses are crooked. I'll take you to the optician along the way so you can have them fixed. I can't have you walking around cockeyed. It's unsightly! I can't have you walking around like that now can I?"

"Give them back, they're fine the way they are! I'm used to them." Leaning forward, Doris squinted, but her son was nothing more than a big blur. "You know how helpless I am without my glasses!"

"Hardly, Mother. It looks like someone punched you." Simon gave her hand a little squeeze. "Don't worry, I'll take good care of you." He put on his best poker face. "You do trust me, don't you?"

"Of course," she muttered. Defeated, Doris sat back and fidgeted with her cane. "What's taking so long? Shouldn't we be there by now?"

Simon snickered. " You're much too uptight. Why can't you just relax for once? Try stressing the positive for a change and maybe you'll feel much better." He pulled the car around a corner and quickened his pace.

Her eyes bulged. "And with good reason! The world is a more dangerous place than it was when I was younger. Nowadays eight-year-olds walk around with loaded guns and they know how to use them!" She folded her flabby arms. "Why, when you and Simon were boys, I refused to let you have cap guns because I thought they were too violent."

"And I still resent you for it." Simon tightened his grip on the steering wheel until his knuckles turned white. "Face it, Mother, you're an easy target."

Doris bit her lip. "Oh, and why is that, just because I'm old? That's not a very fair thing to say."

"It may not be fair, but like it or not it's true." He eased the car over to the curb in front of a decrepit apartment building in a shady part of town and got out. He helped Mother to her feet and led her inside. "Here we are."

She craned her neck and squinted. "This doesn't look like Tiffany's and it's awfully quiet. Where's the hustle and bustle? And why is it so dark in here? Something's wrong."

"Without your glasses on I doubt it looks like much of anything. You might not realize it, but you're the one causing a commotion." His voice was warm, reassuring. He chuckled and pulled her along. "They must have blown a fuse. This way, Mother. Take baby steps and you'll be fine."

She moved her cane back and forth to check for obstructions and proceeded with caution. "Gerald, I'm scared. Where are we?"

"Oh, you'll see soon enough. Careful now, we've got some steep stairs coming up." Simon held her tighter, almost smothering her in his death grip, so she wouldn't topple down headfirst.

Doris clutched his hand—with her firmest grip— overwhelmed by complete helplessness. "How many steps are there? I'm afraid I'll fall!"

"Too many to count. Don't worry, you're in my capable hands, Mother." He led her down the narrow staircase, poorly lit by a dim bulb. "Ready? Down we go. Just put one foot in front of the other and you'll be fine."

She paused for a moment and shook her head. "What's down there, Gerald? I've got a bad feeling about this."

"It's the optician's office." He tugged on her sleeve. "Don't worry, it's perfectly safe. I'll even return your glasses to you once we're downstairs, so you can get your bearings." Simon flashed his winning smile.

"All right, but make it quick, I'm scared to death." Doris bit her lip.

Simon shook his head. "Don't worry, Mother, I won't let anything happen to you, I promise."

She feigned a smile.

He urged her on, "Here we are. Now that wasn't so bad, was it?" Simon unlocked a door and switched on the light.

Doris tapped his leg with her cane. "I almost fell, Gerald."

"But I caught you, just in time, didn't I?" Simon rested a reassuring hand on her shoulder.

"Just barely. It's as if you wanted me to fall!" She frowned.

He shakes his head. "Now you're just letting your imagination get the better of you, Mother. Stop being so paranoid. I insist!"

"I'll try my best. " Her shoes scuffed the smooth, concrete floor. When she squinted, the only thing she could make sense of was the bright light overhead. "Where are my glasses?"

"For the hundredth time, I have them, Mother! You obviously weren't paying attention! I'll hand them over as soon as you sit down!" He squeezed his large hands into trembling fists.

"There's no need to shout, Gerald. I'm not deaf, you know. My ears still work perfectly, but my eyes have seen better days." She shot him a dirty look.

She spread her fingers and held her hands out in front of her; Doris felt her way over to the battered office chair in the center of the cramped space. While she stumbled around, Simon reached for the length of rope resting on the battered desk and gripped it tightly between his fingers.

"Stop wandering around before you hurt yourself, Mother. I wouldn't want anything to happen to you." He rushed over and steered her towards the chair. "Make yourself comfortable, the doctor will be tied up for a while."

Doris gripped the padded armrests and took a seat.

"I'm going to restrain you, so you don't squirm while the doctor examines you. I know how nervous you get around doctors." Simon wrapped the rope around his mother's tiny waist and secured her midsection with a double knot.

"Is that really necessary, Gerald? It seems like a strange precaution. I think I can sit in a chair for a simple eye exam." She started to fidget.

He tied her legs together without bothering to take her cane away. "Better safe than sorry. I wouldn't have it any other way."

"I didn't know you work with doctors." Doris wrinkled her brow.

"There's a lot you don't know about me. That's why we're here, so you can learn a thing or two." Simon tied her arms loosely to the armrests, so as not to damage Mother's delicate wrists then rubbed his hands together. "Ta-da!" He pulled her glasses out of his shirt pocket and slipped them on for her. "I told you I'd return your glasses, safe and sound, good as new. As you can see, I'm a man of my word."

"It's about time!" She pouted as her surroundings come into focus. What she saw made her gasp: Her son brought her to a dank, dark basement with boarded up windows and poor ventilation. "Am I in Hell?" The thought made her shiver.

Simon ran his fingers through his thinning hair. "No, not yet, but don't push your luck."

Doris gawked at him. Her cane rested between her legs, scarcely within reach. "I thought you were going to take me shopping."

"There's been a slight change of plans; I thought this would be more exciting." He winked.

"I'm not having any fun." Doris squirmed in her seat as rough restraints to dug into her tender flesh. "Gerald, untie me this instant!!"

"Is that a threat, Mother? What could you possibly do to me in that chair?" He folded his arms and leaned against the desk.

She lowered her head and took a moment to think. "I can scream." Doris yelled until her voice grew hoarse.

Simon pressed a finger to his lips. "Go ahead and shout all you want. Do you think anyone is going to investigate cries coming from the basement of a run-down building in a bad part of town? Dream on! This is New York City! People could care less!"

Doris immediately stopped screaming while her eyes darted from side to side, unable to focus on anything for more than a few seconds, especially her son. "Why are you doing this to me?" She started to cry.

He walked over to his mother, knelt in front of her, and took her trembling hands in his steady ones. Simon lowered his voice to a whisper, even though it was just the two of them. "Because it's time you realized which one of your sons is more successful. I'll give you a hint, he's standing right in front of you…"

Doris stopped crying. "Gerald, what are you talking about? Of course you're the one. You've got a good job, a beautiful wife, and a wonderful home."

He jumped up and covered his ears with his hands. "I can't believe what I'm hearing, Mother!! You never could tell us apart, could you?!"

She cocked her head and frowned. "What? I—"

"I'm not Gerald!" Simon shouted. His face turned bright red and tendons bulged from his neck like thick wire.

Dumbfounded, his mother blinked. "Well, then who are you?"

"Simon, Gerald's better half!" He started to pace. "Don't tell me you forgot I exist?!"

"Believe me I've tried." Doris puckered her lips. "Who told you Gerald was taking me shopping today?"

He pointed an accusing finger at her. "You mentioned it the other night when I called. You told me he takes you shopping every Saturday afternoon." Simon laughed. "I gave him the afternoon off. I told him you weren't up to the trip."

"Your brother is a successful stockbroker. Did you know that? He always did have a head for numbers. Gerald is the son I could count on." She stared at him, her eyes radiating hatred. "What do you do for a living? Probably something distasteful and illegal."

"You're very clever, Mother. I didn't think you'd catch on so fast, but you surprised me. I'm a hit man and I never miss. In my line of work, it pays to be precise. Missing my mark means missing a big payday. I always get paid." Simon gritted his teeth. "Did you hear me, Mother? I just finished telling you I'm very good at my job. Are you impressed? You should be."

"I heard every last word. Your chosen profession does not please me at all. You kill people for money. I find it utterly repulsive! I suppose you're going to tell me it's all my fault?" Doris raised her eyebrows. "Gerald makes an honest living. Did you know that?"

"Listen to yourself; every other word out of your mouth concerns Gerald! It was the same way when we were little. Always playing favorites!" Simon squeezed his hands into fists. "Mother, you are really trying my patience! That's not a very wise thing to do right now! You taught me how to be cruel."

"How can you say that?" Mother clutched her cane. She had a bright idea.

"I'm just giving credit where credit is due." He walked back to the desk and opened a drawer so slowly it squeaked. "Do you know what I've got in here? Let me wheel you over for a closer look! I know how much you despise a nasty surprise." Struggling against his mother's feet dragging on the floor and her cane, propped precariously between her legs, he finally managed to roll her over to the desk. Loose wheels rattled along the way.

"Probably a knife, a gun or both." Doris shook her head in disgust.

Grinning, Simon pulled a six-inch carving knife out of the cluttered drawer, dangerous and sharp, the blade—worn to a jagged edge and covered with mysterious maroon splotches—shone beneath the naked light bulb. "That's right, Mother, tools of the trade. Devices of torture you never knew existed until now. Sneak a peek." She gasped and turned away. "Come, come, don't be shy—it only hurts the first time." He tugged on Mother's small ears to angle her head for a better view. "And if your mood doesn't improve, I might decide to put some of the more exotic ones to good use." He set the knife down on the desk and reached into the drawer once more.

Doris grudgingly peered inside. "What are those pliers for?"

Simon grabbed a pair and squeezed them shut. "I've pulled a lot of teeth with these. But the people I'm after usually aren't tied up—it's much more challenging if I have to chase them." He tossed the rusty pliers back and rooted around until he found a golden, glimmering hunk of metal with four holes and slid it over his meaty fingers. "Do you know what this is for?"

Mother nodded, not the least bit frightened. "They're called brass knuckles and you can break a man's jaw if you punch him hard enough. I'm sure you have more than once."

Frustrated, Simon yanked them off and slammed the drawer shut. "How could you possibly know that?"

"I've seen a lot of trouble brewing in Hell's Kitchen over the years. I suspect growing up you did, too. It's obviously become your way." Doris gradually loosened the ties that bound her by moving her arms from side to side. Thankfully, Simon was too caught up in his rant to notice.

He snatched the knife from the desk and gripped the smooth, black handle tightly in his hand.

Mother's eyes lit up. "Now I remember you. You always were a troublemaker, competing with Gerald for my attention and usually losing."

"I had no choice, you let me fall by the wayside, like a hasty afterthought. I learned to keep all of my anger inside, until something set me off. Whenever than happens someone gets hurt. I'm very angry, Mother, that's why I'm so good at my job. It's the perfect occupation, it lets me release all of my pent-up aggression." Simon placed the knife dangerously close to Mother's delicate face. "Right now I have your undivided attention. Correct?"

"Yes, now what do you want?" Her eyes were glued to the blade. She started to tremble.

He chuckled. "Well, for starters, I think an apology is in order. Then we'll go from there. Fair enough?"

"If you insist," Mother muttered.

"I do." With one swift motion, Simon slashed Mother's cheek. "Oops! My hand must've slipped!"

Doris flinched as she felt a gush of warm, sticky blood trickle down her neck and dribble onto her good dress. "Simon, you cut me! Why did you do that?!"

"I just told you! Pay attention!" Simon admired Mother's blood as it splattered; the latest addition to the collection of strange stains scattered across the cold concrete. "When I'm angry my hands take on a life of their own. Choose your words carefully. I can't be held responsible for your well-being."

"I'm bleeding, you know and it hurts something awful." She raised her face, trying to slow the flow. "Aren't you going to clean me up?"

"That depends." He watched her intently while he closed in.

"On what?" She hunched her shoulders, bracing herself for the knife's sharp sting a second time.

"Whether or not my mood improves. Right now it's not very good, in case you hadn't noticed." As he spoke, Simon admired his reflection glistening on the blade still tainted with Mother's blood. "Tell me, Mother, how does it feel to be neglected?"

"Simply dreadful." Doris shook her head. Blood flew every-which-way. Simon dodged random splashes of crimson.

"I'm sorry I didn't treat you like Gerald, Simon, but I had my reasons. Your brother was a very demanding child, always wanting to be held, fed, or put down for a nap. Because I was a new mother, I catered to his every whim, I didn't know any better. You seemed content to be tended to whenever I saw fit, which honestly wasn't often enough. In fact, you didn't like to be held the way Gerald did. You'd start to squirm after five minutes, but Gerald would let me lull him to sleep and rock him gently for hours. I guess I got caught up in it all. For that I do apologize. I should have paid you more mind."

"I thought a mother was supposed to love all her children unconditionally…" He wielded the knife again. This time he didn't touch her, but he came much too close for comfort.

Doris sat bolt upright. "I was afraid. I've always been afraid of you." She started to cry again. Tears stung the deep gash on her cheek, but she was much too upset to notice. "Simon, why are you doing this? I'll give you anything you want if you'll untie me and take me home."

Simon bent down to whisper in her ear: "My motive is simple: an eye for and eye. You had your chance to give me the attention I needed early on and you failed miserably. The day of reckoning has arrived." He stood and pulled something compact and gray out of his shirt pocket.

"What have you got there, a fancy gun?" She was almost afraid to look.

"Hardly, Mother. It's an iPhone. Do you mean to tell me you never saw Gerald take an important call on one of these?" Simon turned on his phone and set it down gently on the desk.

Doris shrugged. "I never really noticed."

"That's too bad. Maybe if you paid attention you wouldn't be stuck down here with me right now."

Simon clasped his hand over Mother's mouth before she could reply. Then he picked up the phone and pressed a button. When he set it down again, Mother heard it ring a shrill chirping that set her on edge until her prodigal son answered. "Hello?" Gerald sounded anxious, his voice distant.

"Oh, sorry. Did I catch you at a bad time, Gerald? I know you're a busy man." Simon chuckled.

Mother bit his hand, drawing blood. He stifled a scream and pinched her cheek so she wouldn't squirm.

Gerald sighed. "As a matter of fact I was in the middle of something very—"

"Important? What I have is far more precious, trust me." He snickered.

"Who is this?" he asked, really pissed.

Despite his efforts, Mother nipped Simon's hand again. He pulled it away to inspect for serious damage and found a small cut, an unwanted distraction.

"Gerald, you have to help me! Simon's got me tied up in the basement and he's cut me with a knife! There's no telling what he'll do next!" Doris screamed, frantic to escape.

Gerald groaned. "Mother, where are you?"

"I'm right here, brother." Simon took a deep breath and gagged Mother with the bloody rag to keep her quiet.

"Did you hurt her?" he asked, concerned.

Simon snickered. "Not too badly, but that may change soon."

"What do you want?!" Gerald shouted.

"Come on, don't play dumb with me!" Simon slammed his fist down on the desk. "If you don't come up with one million dollars by midnight, Mother's history!"

Gerald cleared his throat. "Where do you want it?"

"Meet me in the basement of my building in Hell's Kitchen. Do you know it?" Simon barked into the phone.

"Yes…I'm on my way…You'll get your money…Just don't hurt her…" Gerald's voice faded into static.

Simon ended the call and slipped the phone back in his shirt pocket.

He turned to Mother and snarled, "If I take that gag off, do you promise to behave?" Simon towered over her. Simon's hands rested on his hips.

Wide-eyed, Doris slowly nodded. She slipped one of her shoes off and wriggled out from under the ropes.

He removed the bloody rag stuffed into Mother's mouth carefully, doing his best to avoid her vicious bite.

"Simon, could you help me get my shoe back on? It slipped off." She bent down and wriggled her fingers to stress her effort. "I can't seem to reach it."

"Of course, Mother. It's the least I can do." He blushed. "I wouldn't want you to hurt yourself. Sit back and I'll fix it for you." Without giving it much thought, Simon set the knife down on the cold concrete and gently slipped his mother's tiny foot back into her sensible shoe.

"That's very thoughtful, Simon." Doris reached over and patted her son's broad shoulder.

Simon leered at her. "I try my best."

Doris raised her arms and swung her cane hard. A hollow whack connected hickory with Simon's thick skull—he grunted and hit the floor with a soft thud—splinters skidded across cold concrete.

"You always let your guard down when you were a boy and I told you it would get you into trouble someday. Such a pity you didn't listen!" Mother's green eyes twinkled as she slowly got to her feet and cautiously picked up the knife resting next to Simon. It felt heavy and awkward between her frail fingers—an impossible burden to bear—she struggled to hold it steady, with both hands, and tip-toed over to the spot where her son rested—bruised and beaten—on cold concrete dotted with splotches of his warm blood.

Simon regarded Mother with a vacant stare as the blood that trickled out of his mouth formed a slick pool at her feet.

"Just look at the awful mess you've made! You always were a careless boy, smashing my precious bone China, just to watch it break!" She twisted her hands until they turned bright red. "Gerald was such a neat freak, everything had to be in its place or he'd have a fit!" Doris shook her head. "It's such a shame you didn't turn out like your brother. I'm very disappointed."

He reached out to grab her ankle and missed. "Don't leave me like this, Mother! I ache all over!" Simon slurred his plea.

"Serves you right! Now you know how I feel!" Doris ground her heel into his hand. Simon yanked it away and shrieked. He crawled to the foot of the stairs.

"I should have smothered you when you were a baby! I won't make the same mistake twice!" Doris looked at her sniveling son, and smiled. "You've been very bad, Simon! It's time for you learn the value of discipline!" She grabbed him by the scruff of his neck, swiped the knife from the desk and strained to lift it above her head. She aimed for his heart and plunged the blade deep into his chest several times. Simon opened his mouth to scream. Too shocked to make a sound, he clutched his ruined chest and lay perfectly still.

Being careful not to trip on the remnants of her cane, Doris got down on her knees and checked her son's wrist for a pulse. She laughed when she didn't find one and got slowly to her feet. Doris leaned on the wall, and shuffled over to the door. She fumbled with the locks, yanked it open, and climbed the stairs slowly.

Gerald waited for her near the top, his timing impeccable, as always.

"Are you all right, Mother? What happed to Simon?" He stared at his brother's body sprawled out on the floor near the stairs. "I got here as fast as I could—traffic is murder this time of day." He took her by the hand and brought her over to the navy blue Audi parked at the curb.

"I'm bleeding, Gerald. Simon gave me a nasty cut." Doris pointed to her face.

Always the perfect gentleman, Gerald pulled a crisp, white handkerchief out of his pant's pocket and pressed it against her cheek, to help ease her pain. "I'd better get you to the hospital. You're going to need stitches." He looked her over. "What happened to your cane?"

"I whacked your brother over the head with it." She stared at her son. "I'll have you know he threatened my life and I killed him for it."

Gerald shook his head and helped her into the car. "Why don't I take you shopping after they make you all better at the hospital? To help you forget all about this nastiness."

Doris nodded, slowly, anxious to forget. "I'd enjoy that, Gerald. Will you take me to Tiffany's?"

"I'll take you anywhere you want to go. I promise." He laid a reassuring hand on her shoulder.

"You always were a good boy." Doris smiled and buckled her seat belt.

"You taught me well." Gerald winked and drove off.

Amy Grech has sold over 100 stories to various anthologies and magazines including: *Apex Magazine, Beat to a Pulp: Hardboiled, Dead Harvest, Detectives of the Fantastic, Volume II, Expiration Date, Fear on Demand, Funeral Party 2, Inhuman Magazine, Needle Magazine, Reel Dark, Shrieks and Shivers from the Horror Zine, Space & Time, The Horror Within, Under the Bed,* and many others. New Pulp Press http://www.newpulppress. com recently published her book of noir stories, *Rage and Redemption in Alphabet City.*

She has stories forthcoming in *Fright Mare.* Amy is an Active Member of the Horror Writers Association and lives in Brooklyn. Visit her website: http://www. crimsonscreams.com. Follow Amy on Twitter: http:// twitter.com/amy_grech.

How long can Leha stand on her principles when her world collapses around her?

Kin
By Rayne Hall

(loosely based on a Shakespeare drama)

Widow Leha rubbed her cold-stiffened hands against her cheeks. After six nights in a makeshift shelter of broken beams and fir branches, would she ever feel warm again?

"Come, now." The neighbour boy, twelve-year-old Jehanzeb, pulled her sleeve. "It's our duty to find food." Carrying his father's bronze scimitar strapped to his back, he seemed to have grown taller and straighter than she remembered.

The Mighty Ones had swept most of the village down the slope into the ravine, teaching the sinners a forceful lesson. But they had also smashed Leha's home, turning it into a rubble of mudbrick, studded with splintered roof beams, soaked with spilled olive oil and animal blood.

Thirty years ago, a young man had promised Leha to build her the most beautiful house on this spot if she would wed him. With his own hands he had created a two-storey jewel with a veranda, a livestock stable, and living quarters. It had been a perfect home, for many years alive with children's laughter. Now it was gone.

She owned nothing but the nightdress on her body, the small gold drops in her ear, and a curtain to wrap around her against the cold.

Mighty Ones, why have you struck my home with the same blow as those of the sinners? I did not need this lesson. I have always listened and obeyed your laws.

But arguing with the gods was futile.

"We're blessed, because the gods have chosen us for their protection," she told the boy. "We must remember to thank them with proper prayers, and prove ourselves worthy of their favour in everything we do." She drew her embroidered curtain around her head against the biting morning wind.

"We're blessed because we have kin. It's not the walls around us, but the family around us that make our home," Jehanzeb quoted with earnest pride. "This is written in the Wisdom Scrolls. I've learnt it in Temple School. I'm blessed because I have four sisters alive, and my sisters are blessed because they have me. And you have your three daughters."

"Two daughters," Leha corrected firmly. "I have two fine grown-up daughters. Only two." Once there had been three children in that house, but the youngest, like the foul flesh of a bruised apple, had to be cut out before it could spoil the rest of the fruit.

"Let's go." She set off.

A steady drizzle cloaked everything in dampness, and the wind drove a chill deep into the bones. Leha and Jehanzeb marched briskly. With every step on the steep-sloping, rubble-strewn path, pain stabbed into her ageing knees.

That first night under the cold stars, Leha said her prayers and Jehanzeb stroked his scimitar before they huddled together in a hollow. They shared a blanket and the warmth of their bodies. The biting chill drove searing pain into Leha's joints. She wanted to weep.

Why, Mighty Ones, are you tormenting me so? Have I not always served you well? Have I not cut my own daughter out of the family, obeying your divine will, and wiped her name from memory? Have I not been good?

As soon as the first fingers of dawn touched the sky, Leha and Jehanzeb rose to keep searching a region unscathed by divine wrath. Surely in Ain Muzab they would get food and shelter, and help for those left behind.

But the further they trekked, the greater the devastation grew. Landslides had carried away the mountain track, ripped the bridges from their foundations, covered the paths with rubble and mud. Mountain after mountain had its snow-capped peaks cracked, its sloping pastures ripped open, its insides exposed as gaping wounds. The fist of disaster had shattered the whole world.

Clusters of fresh grave mounds appeared like mushrooms everywhere, and still more dead were being pulled from the rubble. People carried hunger in their eyes, and the injured moaned softly.

Leha's chest brimmed with pity for their suffering. "I have no food." She showed her empty palms. "But I will pray to the Mighty Ones for you."

"Prayers won't fill my stomach," a woman grumbled, "nor rebuild my home."

A flock of youngsters descended on Leha, tore at her curtain-shawl, and yelled with triumph at the sight of her earrings. "Gold! She has gold drops in her ears!" They would have ripped the drops from her ears had Jehanzeb not drawn his scimitar.

From then on, she kept her ears covered, and her face averted, to avoid attention. Suffering had turned these people into shameless beasts who no longer saw right from wrong. They might kill wanderers to rob them of the flesh they carried on their bones.

Every day she expected to reach the regions where disaster had not struck, but silence and suffering spread everywhere. What if even Ain Muzab was struck? What if Mahlega and Gonila had been hurt? Hunger gnawed at her stomach, and worry at her heart, and it grew hard to keep up with her companion's cheer.

It took seven days of desperate marching, with nothing in their stomachs but water and grass, before they neared Ain Muzab. Hordes of desperate relief seekers had stamped out a winding, narrow, slippery path. People were trying to reach the remnants of the road below, while others were returning home, carrying bales and sacks on their heads with whatever useful items they had been able to beg, buy or scavenge.

"Go back home, there's no help in Ain Muzab!" an angry man shouted. "The officials are worse than warlords."

One woman thrust a basket at her. "Look at this. That's what they gave me. Five bunches of dates. That's all I got for my whole family, and I tell you, I walked three days to get there." When Leha peeked at the basket, the woman snatched it away as if fearing theft.

"Tell me, good woman," Leha begged. "How is the area around the market? Does the schoolhouse still stand?"

"You won't believe the prices they charge for bread and yoghurt now! I tell you, it's robbery, that's what it is."

"My daughters live there, I must know," Leha begged. "My eldest, with her husband and children, on the north end of the market. He's an official. Have you met him? And Gonila is the teacher, she lives in the schoolhouse. Please tell me, does the schoolhouse stand?"

"Robbery, I tell you, these officials should be hanged."

No one offered information about what mattered most, so Leha walked on. At last, the town came within sight.

The vision tempted her to wish she was blind. Even from the distance, she smelled death, sickening and sweet. Half the mountain had tumbled into the valley, smothering half the town and smashing the rest. Landmarks lay in shattered ruins.

Squinting against the midday sun, she tried to discern patterns where roads had been. Yes, that was the road that led from the market to the temple. Yes, some houses stood - battered and broken, but still proud amidst the rubble and dust. And yes, yes, yes! There was the one she had given Mahlega as her dowry. The schoolhouse also stood like a solitary tower amidst the decay.

Joy drove her on. Her girls were safe. They would embrace her in their homes.

Once she and her husband had owned three houses, two in town, and one in the mountain village. They'd been merchants and had lived in town. But then she'd sold one house to finance her second daughter's education, and given Mahlega the other as a dowry. She'd retired to the small house in the mountains, the one she loved most. Eventually she had meant to give this third house to her favourite daughter, the lovely Komal – but – no, she wouldn't think about that ungrateful girl.

But on the walk down the steep track, thoughts of Komal pierced her like needles. Had the girl survived the earthquake? How was she faring, with a small child and no husband?

"She's no longer my kin," Leha said, unaware that she was speaking aloud.

Jehanzeb raised an arm like a lecturing priest. "I learnt at Temple School that mercy blesses those who give as well as those who take. And the Book of Crones says that even when kin are like spittle, we must keep swallowing them lest we die of thirst."

"The Book of Crones also says: Don't do any good to the bad, and don't expect good from the bad," Leha countered. "Komal brought shame on the family. She disgraced us by getting with child. Not even by a man who would marry her, but by a passing stranger. By casting her out I acted righteous."

"The Seventh Scroll of Wisdom says that kin need to stick to kin like skin to the flesh."

Leha snorted. "Save your proverbs for school. This is real life, and you'll soon find you have some serious lessons to learn."

"I know. I'm the man of the family now, and won't go back to school."

"My two real daughters love me and give me nothing but pride and joy."

"I always liked Komal best," Jehanzeb said. "She taught me to read even before I went to Temple School."

Leha's heart ached at the foul memory. Komal had been a kind girl, and clever, too. Cleverer even than

Gonila. A real scholar, the best girl in her class, she had always helped children whose parents couldn't afford the school fees. Who would have thought that this compassionate, pious daughter would choose the path of sin and disgrace?

"It says in Scroll fourteen: Drive out the rat lest it brings the plague to your home." That would show this precocious boy that she, too, had an education. "Even her sisters agreed that she had to go! I was compassionate even as I cast her out. I let her take her clothes and gave her a blanket."

"Clothes and a blanket," Jehanzeb repeated in a tone of wonderment which made her generosity sound mean.

They crossed the river by the only surviving bridge which hung by frayed ropes.

The rain had finally ceased. Families huddled, hollow-eyed, coughing and sneezing, around fires that didn't want to burn in the still-damp air. Children with matted hair, blood-encrusted clothes and runny noses held out their hands and bare feet towards the flames, begging for warmth. Leha's heart lurched with pity, and she thanked the Mighty Ones that her own ordeal would be over soon. She wouldn't need to surrender to this misery.

The upper story of Mahlega's home showed a crack in the wall, and part of the roof had tumbled in, but there was life inside.

"Come in, come in," Leha urged her young companion. "You need a hot meal and a rest as much as I do."

"I think not." He gazed at his hands, flexed his fingers. "I'll join the relief queues while they still have food."

He sneaked away before she could reply.

The door opened a crack. "Oh Mother, it's you. I'm so glad you're here." Mahlega undid the chain and pulled her mother in. "Come quickly, so the heat doesn't escape."

She bolted the door before drawing Leha into a jasmine-scented embrace and shouted back into the living room, "All's well now, Mother has come."

The place smelled of sandalwood incense, hot mint and spicy stew. The warm air caressed Leha's cheeks.

"The place is a mess, I'm afraid," Mahlega apologised, "All of us living on the ground floor now, because the roof has caved in. The window parchments have ripped, so it's awfully cold, even with the rugs nailed across."

"It feels cosy to me," Leha assured her. After sleeping outdoors, this home was a paradise of warmth.

Mahlega shoved a stray strand of hair out of her face. "The well has dried up, so I have to walk all the way to the river to get water, and I have to filter and boil it because it's not clean. The youngest has a broken leg and won't keep it still, all my painted clay bowls got smashed. You can't get decent stuff in the market, nobody says when they'll repair our homes, all the authorities send is pickled olives and dried dates, and worn clothes, would you believe it? Summer tunics, useless in this weather, and smelly and stained." Mahlega paused in her whines to let out a deeper sigh. "I'll boil up a pot of water on the stove, so you can have a warm wash, though we really don't have much firewood left, and I'll sort out some dry clothes."

Leha slipped into the curtained-off wash corner. Warmth prickled her fingers with welcome pain. She took her time to rinse away the travel dust and the weariness, enjoying every drop of warmth on her flesh. Then she joined the family for the evening meal. Mahlega's husband spoke the prayers in the resonant voice of a skilled preacher, thanking the Mighty Ones for his job, his income, his good health and that of his family. "And especially thanks for sending Leha to us in this time of need."

Leha savoured the buttered couscous, the spicy beans, the fragrant mint tea.

Again, Mahlega apologised for the untidiness and reduced comforts of the place, and Leha assured her she didn't mind at all. "Up in the village, people have nothing left, not even a room or a stove or a change of clothes. They're starving and freezing."

Mahlega patted her hair which was piled high on her head and fastened with glittery barrettes. "This place is a mess. I can't put up with this much longer. We can't live on the ground floor with six people in just two rooms."

Leha filled her bowl with couscous for the third time, helped herself to more lentils, and sent another grateful silent prayer to the Mighty Ones for the food.

The twins were quarrelling, the youngest sneezed and whined, and the oldest boy shouted from the bench, "I'm fed up with staying here. This leg itches. Why can't I have it fixed properly?"

One of the twins banged his spoon on the table. "Why can't we have new clothes for the Festival of the Dancing Souls? All our friends are getting new clothes."

"Mighty Ones, Mahlega, can't you keep them quiet?" the husband said. "I deserve to eat my meal in peace."

She lowered her lids. "Yes, husband."

93

To Leha, he said, "I've got my hands full at work, you can't imagine. All the corpses still lying under the rubble – I'm the one who has to find people to dig them out. And all those refugees! They come from the mountains and expect to be housed and fed. I'm dealing with supplies, distribution, health hazards, beggars, robbery, all day long, and then I come home and I have to listen to more squabbles."

"The government doesn't help," Mahlega said. "You'd think they'd give us some real help, like money to fix the roof. But all we get is dried dates, dates and more dates. Not even fine ones, but the low grade normally used for animal fodder. Same as the beggars."

Leha put down her spoon. "Up in the village, people would be grateful for the dates. I've met a woman on the way here, she walked for days just to get some dates for her family. There's a boy, Jehanzeb, who came down with me. You may remember him, Mahlega. I wonder if we could –"

"Surely you don't plan to dump that urchin on us!"

"He's an obnoxious wise-cracker, but he's polite and kind, and he always helps me milk -" Leha corrected herself. "He always used to help me milk the cows and muck out the stables."

"You paid him for that, didn't you?"

"He also helped me on the way here. I couldn't have done without him."

"He's a pest, always scrounging. He'd like it fine to come in here and eat our food."

"He's a good boy," Leha insisted. "He's always doing what is right."

"I tell you," the husband said, "he's after free handouts like everyone else. They come and want everything for free and give nothing. Not like you." He leant across the table and pressed both hands around Leha's. "I'm so glad you've come. Now we can move into the house by the temple."

Leha frowned. "What house by the temple?"

"Your house by the Temple of the Divine Mercy. I checked it this morning, and it's sound, without even a crack. I'll help you evict the tenants."

"I don't own that house any more. I sold it years ago to pay for Gonila's education."

He dropped her hands. "I can't believe it. Mahlega, did you know about this?"

Mahlega lowered her eyes. "Now that she mentions it, I remember, Gonila's school fees were expensive."

"Almost exactly the same value as your dowry," Leha pointed out. "Which included this house. Have I not always treated you both with absolute fairness?"

Mahlega focused on mashing the vegetables in her bowl. "It's just that we would really need that house now."

"Because this one is in a state," her husband said. "I don't have the money to get the fallen roof repaired." His eyes pierced Leha like robbers' daggers, demanding payment.

"My own house is gone," she said. "And with it all I possessed. Until I can find someone to rebuild it for me, I'll have to live with you."

They looked at her aghast.

"Out of the question," her son-in-law said. "I can't have you live here, with six people in two rooms already."

The eldest said, "She can sleep in the bed with Mama, and you sleep on the floor with us."

Silence soaked the air. Mahlega heaped more couscous in her husband's already piled bowl.

95

"Why aren't you sleeping on the floor with us, Papa?" one of the twins asked. The youngest piped up, "I want to sleep in the bed with Grandma."

"That's enough!" He slammed a fist on the table, making the bowls jump. "I will not have disobedience in my house. Mahlega, can't you teach them to behave?"

She ladled another spoon of couscous on his heap. The embarrassed flush of her face almost matched her deep pink shawl. "I'm sorry, Mother, that's how it is," she muttered. "Of course you're welcome to drop in for a meal now and then."

"And I'll assist you with advice. I'll tell you which office to go to queue for a place in a tent," her husband said. "Better go soon, the queues are bound to be long at night, and when I'm not there to oversee matters, things are bound to go wrong."

Swallowing her disappointment, Leha forced a smile. "Let's go straight away."

"I can't go to the office outside my regular duty hours. I mean, what would my superiors think?" His nose crinkled. "It's not that I'm ashamed of being seen with you, not really, but this is something you can do yourself."

"I see." The spicy beans suddenly tasted stale.

He crossed his arms over his chest. "I've worked all day, I've dealt with everyone's problems, my head aches, I'm tired."

Mahlega stroked his arm, soothing. "You deserve a rest, dear, you do."

Leha rose. "I have walked all the way from the village to come here. Five days. I'm aching and bruised. I don't have proper clothes, and my shoes have holes. And this is all I get?"

"Of course not." He glanced at her through narrowed eyes. "I won't expect my mother-in-law to walk from my house in rags." He turned to his wife. "Find her something, won't you?"

"Keep the clothes you have on," Mahlega said. "And you can have my old boots, they still have a lot of wear in them. And a blanket."

"Get her a bowl of couscous," the husband instructed. "No, give her two."

The door clanked shut behind Leha. A sharp breeze slapped her cheeks and blew venom into her eyes. She wrapped her new shawl – her daughter's old shawl, laden with red ruffles and silvery tassels, and rich with the smell of jasmine – tightly around her head.

Mighty Ones, let these people taste the fruit of bitterness. Turn their own children against them, let them feel what it means to be cast aside.

Fortunately, she had another daughter, one who truly loved her and who was not poisoned by a husband's ambitions.

Fields of rubble had replaced roads, and the day's drizzle had turned the broken bricks and dust into dark red mud. Rats scurried, chased by hungry boys. Small girls dug with bare fingers for earth worms and grubs. Lehah walked fast towards the schoolhouse, skirting around broken wall segments and stepping across slabs of stone, her head lowered against the wind's bite.

Someone blocked her way. "Leha."

It was scimitar-armed Jehanzeb with a world-wisdom in his eyes that had not been there days ago.

"Oh, Leha, I'm so sorry. They've sent you away. But they've given you clothes and a blanket."

She straightened. Pity was no welcome gift. "And couscous." Then the tears burst through.

He pushed the scimitar back and wrapped his arms around her, like a grown man protecting a woman in his care.

Stiffening, she pulled herself from his sheltering embrace. "How did you fare? Your hands are empty."

"I got dates and milk, the Mighty Ones be thanked, and a sack of flour and three blankets."

"That's not much for a family of five."

"It's more than I had yesterday. And the Mighty Ones have sent me in the path of women who go the same way home. They let their mules carry my stuff, and in return I protect them from robbers on the way."

Leha looked at the slight boy and tried to see a man. "They'll be glad to have a man to protect them on the way. Without you, those robbers would have killed me."

He coughed and flexed his fingers, the way he used to when begging for a sweet. "I've seen someone we both used to know. She lives -"

Leha cut him off. "I'm going to the schoolhouse."

"Oh, I remember Gonila. The very clever one. She won prizes at school and went to college, didn't she? Although when my sisters asked her to help them with their writing, she called them dirty brats."

"She was probably just too busy with her studies, or she would have helped you. Gonila's a nice girl, and she's very independent. She earns her own money and doesn't need a man. Give your sisters my blessings. I'll pray for you all."

The schoolhouse stood, with its downstairs classroom and the teacher's accommodation in the wooden upper story.

Gonila, as always dressed in sensible grey, beamed. "Mother, what a wonderful surprise! Today, all my dearest wishes come true. Seeing you once more was one of them. How are things in the village?"

"Bad." Briefly, Leha described the situation. "You are blessed that you still have a home." She took off her shawl and glanced around the clean, sparse room. Gonila had always lived simply, but the fireplace was cold. No chairs, no rugs, no bed, not even a sleeping mat offered comfort.

"Yes, I'm blessed. The earthquake didn't touch me." Gonila didn't invite her to sit on the floor, and remained standing. "And even better! You know I applied to go to statecraft school, and was turned down, together with five thousand other candidates? Another woman from Ain Muzab was selected. But she got killed in the earthquake, so there's a vacancy, and I'm taking her place. I'll be one of the four only females! Opportunity knocked on my door, and I was ready. I'll be an important woman, and never depend on anyone."

"I've always known you were a clever one! I'll be so proud of you. But what happened to your furniture? Have you given it away to needy people?"

"I sold it, to raise money for the journey. That was one of today's blessings. A single buyer took it all for a good price. Are you staying with Mahlega?"

"No." Leha told her a toned-down version of how she had been treated. "So I'll come to stay with you."

"Oh." Awkward silence stretched the distance. "Oh, Mother. That's what I've been telling you. I'm going away to study at statecraft school. I'm leaving now. The caravan is already waiting." She shouldered the basket. "I'm in a hurry, really. Come and see me off."

"And the room?"

"It goes with the job, of course. The officials will appoint someone before the day is out."

Chills crawled across Leha's skin. "You're giving up this home? I can't even stay here tonight?"

"Yes. Come now." Impatience swung in her voice.

"But I need somewhere to stay. You can't leave now."

"I can't miss this once-in-a-lifetime chance. I'm sure an opportunity will arise for you, too, if you stay open-minded. Maybe Mahlega's husband can get you a place in the tent camp for refugees." She looked pained. "I'm sorry I can't offer you hospitality, but I have to vacate this room. Believe me, if I could help you, I would." Her brow furrowed, then brightened. "You can have my cooking pot! I won't have to do my own cooking at statecraft school, and it's solid copper."

"Why can't you stay a few days longer?"

"You have no idea, do you? This is the only caravan leaving town for who knows how long, and if I don't act, someone else will snap up the study place." She rubbed the side of her neck. "It's going to be difficult. Even with the scholarship, life in the city is going to be expensive. I had to pay out all my savings to the caravan leader. With your house gone, I suppose you can't give me much support, but even a little would help." She eyed the gold drops in Leha's ears.

Leha pulled them out and tossed them at her daughter's feet. "Payment for your cooking pot." She rose. "The Mighty Ones be with you."

100

She let the door click shut behind her. The chill bit at her cheeks.

Jehanzeb leaned against the trunk of a splintered tree, as if he had expecting her to come out.

"A cooking pot? Nice." He hoisted her blanket over one shoulder and grabbed the basket. "You have another daughter. I've seen..."

"No!"

"I'll show you where to queue for food." He cleared his throat. "But then I'll have to be off. Duty calls. I have women to protect on the journey, and sisters to care for at home. Duty fulfilled with pride tastes sweeter than honey, says the Book of Crones."

"Wait, Jehanzeb!" She pressed her basket at him. "Take this: two bowls of couscous. You'll need them on your long journey." She waved away his protests. "I had a large meal at Mahlega's house."

The air smelled of damp wood smoke and human misery. Standing in a line behind a hundred dejected people, Leha watched the sun sliding towards the western peaks. With Jehanzeb, the last link to the world she had known was gone, and with it, the last kindness and cheer.

"Hello?" a soft female voice beside Leha said. She hardened her features and pretended not to hear. She had nothing to give to beggars, and if anyone had come to gloat at her misery, she would not give them the chance.

"Hello?" Someone tugged at her shawl. She jerked away. Then a baby gurgled.

"Mother?" A small woman, draped in a demure blue shawl, a baby in her arms - Komal. "Jehanzeb told us you were here, Mother."

"He had no right," Leha snarled. "And I'm not your mother. You're no daughter of mine. Go away."

The baby, drawn by the glittery tassels, clawed its fingers into her shawl.

Komal glanced along the queue. "I see Mahlega has not welcomed you any more than us. I'm sorry."

With pursed lips, Leha looked her up and down. Then she flicked her chin at the baby. "So you got another. Picked up from another travelling man?"

She pulled the shawl from the child's fingers and spun on her heels. With her chin held in high dignity, she stared ahead, shutting out all memory of the family disgrace.

When she reached the front of the queue, a bored official under a wind-flapping awning wrote her name on a waxed wooden tablet. "Name? Status? Age? Regular resident or visitor?"

"My name's Leha. I'm a widow, 48 winters. I've walked five days to get here. Our village is destroyed. I've lost my home, my animals, my clothes..."

"Visitor." He scratched a mark on his tablet. "No aid has been allocated to visitors at this stage. Next!"

She held up her palms. "Please, listen, good sir. I have nowhere to stay..."

His thin nose wrinkled as if he had smelled a chamberpot. "We don't have enough resources for residents. We can't take in beggars."

Wind shook the awning and rattled the poles. "Please, I need shelter from the weather. A dormitory, a tent, anything."

He shrugged narrow shoulders and flicked a speck of dust off his sleeve. "Go back to where you come from. Next!"

Clutching the blanket and the cooking pot, she stumbled across debris-strewn paths in search of a sheltering corner. Shacks of splintered timber leaned against walls, battered by gusts. Children scavenged the rubble heaps for anything useful, while old folks huddled around sparse fires, burning broken beds. Winds howled through the ruins and spat spark-laden smoke into Leha's face. The cold seeped through her clothes and flesh right into her bones.

Every sheltering spot was already claimed by hostile people who drove Leha off with yells and stones.

At the temple, staff-armed priests fended off refugees, shouting, "This is a place of worship, not a doss house!"

Rumbles of thunder rolled across the darkening sky. Lightning flashes flickered, and fierce air blasts threatened to thrash what the earthquake had spared. Improvised shelters tumbled. Men cursed.

The turbulence of the thunderstorm echoed the whirling distress in her soul.

Mighty Ones, why have you cast me into this violent night? I know now that I was foolish, that my eyes needed opening, that I needed to taste the salty truth. I believed in gratitude where there was only greed, and in love where the hearts were cold. The daughters I cherished did not exist save in the dreams of a fond old woman. Like dogs they are, like rats, like tigers! The bite of their betrayal stings worse than a serpent's tooth. Tonight, I've ripped them from my heart, and I have learnt not to trust again. But, Mighty Ones, I have learnt that lesson, so shelter me now, and call off the storm!

Heaven raged on, rumbling and roiling. Thunder ripped the sky. Gusts pushed and punched Leha as she staggered in search of cover.

"Mother."

Komal again. As if Leha had not enough problems, now the Mighty Ones had send that shameless girl to gloat. If the daughters who owed her everything had treated her with contempt, what would the one who had cause to hate her do?

"Our home is gone," Komal shouted over the roaring wind. "Omar has built a small shelter from timbers."

"I have nothing to give!" Leha yelled back.

"Compared with what you're used to, our shack is poor, but..."

"Whatever you're hoping for, you won't get it. I have no property left, no animals, no jewellery."

The storm's angry fist slammed into Leha and tossed her against the temple wall. The copper pot clanked.

Komal pulled at her harm. "Mighty Ones, Mother, come out of this weather, just for one night!"

Lightning cracked and split the sky. The whole earth quivered.

Leha nodded curtly, dropped her pride and gathered the blanket close to her. "I'll have a look."

They climbed across red rubble to a patch where people had stacked debris into shacks which shivered under the onslaught.

Only one of them stood solid and straight.

"Omar, Omar!" Komal called. "I've found her. Sayyed, your grandmother has come at last. Come in, Mother."

Leha ducked into the lightless place. A man rose. In the near-darkness, he looked dirty, his arms bloody and chafed, his face smeared with grime and sweat. He bowed. "You honour us with your visit. We hoped you'd seek us out, but Jehanzeb said you didn't want to."

A child of three or four traipsed forward and clutched arm around Leha's leg. "Are you my grandmother?"

Gently, Leha shook the burden off her leg and stepped away from it. This had to be the bastard, conceived when the shameless girl had lain with a passing stranger. She would not acknowledge a bond.

She studied the hut. Salvaged beams were assembled with sharp precisions, and stones held together with clay. Wind still whipped through the door opening, but the construction was solid and would withstand the ferocious force.

"Not bad," she said.

Komal beamed as if she had received a great compliment. "Omar is a master carpenter! He's lost his tools, of course, but he still has his skill. When the other people just sat and moaned about kismet, Omar got to work. It's a fine place, isn't it?"

"I'll improve it tomorrow," Omar said proudly. "I cannot give my wife and children a smart home, but I can keep them safe. It won't be a palace, but I promise it'll be the nicest home in the neighbourhood." He laughed. "Not that there's much competition from those shacks."

Heat rushed to Leha's cheeks. That's what her husband had told her, when he had first courted her. "I'm poor," he had said. "But I'll build a house for you. It won't be a palace, but it will be the nicest home in the neighbourhood. Not that there's much competition on this mountain."

"I'd offer you tea, but I don't have a pot," Komal said.

So this was what the invitation was about! She clanked the copper vessel at the young woman's feet. "Keep it, and don't bother me again."

Omar blocked her entrance. "You honour us by staying the night, Mother. May I call you Mother?"

Outside, the wind howled. Wood clattered and women wailed as poor shacks collapsed. Someone squealed with pain.

"I know it's not a fine building like the one you're used to," he said. "But we're kin. In times like this, it's important for kin to stick together, isn't it?"

Holding on to her pride was getting difficult. "Are you the father of those brats?"

The smile on his face collapsed. She had succeeded in unsettling him at last.

Komal finished pouring water from a bucket into the pot. "Omar and I met the year after Sayyed's birth. He's the best father I could wish for my children."

The serene smile settled on Omar's face again. "When I married, I got not only the best wife in the world, but a fine son. Now we have a girl as well. And if you stay with us, we'll be a real family."

Leha put her blanket down. "All right. If you'll have me, I'll stay for the night." She trusted the darkness to hide the moisture in her eyes.

Hope, gratitude, contempt and guilt churned in her chest, stirring a storm of confusion. She closed her eyes, clutching the wall for support. The Mighty Ones, it seemed, had another lesson for her, a lesson she could not yet understand but might learn if she stayed in this humble shack.

"That husband doesn't seem too bad," she muttered to Komal. "And the shelter he's built isn't bad either, considering the neighbourhood."

She wanted to say, "Maybe you're not too bad either, considering your sisters", but tiredness clawed into her brain, and she dropped to the floor with exhaustion. Perhaps she would stay more than one night.

Rayne Hall has published more than fifty books in several languages under several pen names with several publishers in several genres, mostly fantasy, horror and non-fiction. She is the author of the dark-epic fantasy novel *Storm Dancer,* the creepy horror story collection *Thirty Scary Tales,* and the bestselling *Writer's Craft* series (*Writing Fight Scenes, Writing Scary Scenes, Writing About Villains, Writing About Magic, Writing Dark Stories* and more) as well as the publisher and editor of the *Ten Tales* fantasy anthologies.

Having lived in Germany, China, Mongolia and Nepal, she has settled in St Leonards, England, where she enjoys reading, gardening and long walks along the seashore. She shares her home with a black cat adopted from the cat shelter. Sulu likes to lie on the desk and snuggle into Rayne's arms when she's writing.

You can follow her on Twitter http://twitter.com/ RayneHall where she posts advice for writers, funny cartoons and cute pictures of her cat. To see her books, go to viewAuthor.at/RayneHall . Rayne's website is here: http://raynehallauthor.wix.com/rayne-hall

To find out about new book releases, workshops, writing contests and events, sign up for the newsletter: http://eepurl.com/boqJzD

Michelangelo is a great artist but will he pay his biscotti bill?

Burning Michelangelo
By Annemarie Schiavi Pedersen

The young artist shuffling into her bakery drew pictures the way David brought down the giant, like it was the two of them against the world. From behind the counter, a sharp pain hit Simona in the stomach. She swore Michelangelo slung a rock at her.

Hurrying to serve morning customers in line before him, she braced for their daily fight. He'd better have her money today, because if he didn't pay his debt, and pronto, she'd be spending the rest of her days rotting in Le Stinche, the debtor's prison that loomed like the inner layer of hell in the center of the city of Florence.

She leaned across the counter, sneering in his face. "Bon giorno, Signor Buonarroti."

"Tre biscotti," Michelangelo said, eyes skimming the tray of freshly baked pistachio cookies.

She hunted for her three worst biscuits, and then pressed each one into his palm. She hated to admit it, but the pictures he created with those of his hands of his were nothing if not Godly.

She presented her own hand, wiggling her fingers, rocking on her toes, waiting for him to pay. He bit into a cookie. Finally, she demanded, "Nine baiocchi."

He shoved a second biscuit in his mouth before digging in his leather satchel. Turning the purse inside out, he shrugged. "No money."

To keep her hand from reaching down his throat to fetch back her biscuit, Simona pounded her fist on the marble counter. "Pay your debt! Six scudi, plus nine pennies for today."

Step-by-step he backed up. Swiftly he was out the door.

Slapping the counter, Simona cried, "Son-of-a-bitch." She pushed aside customers, flying out the front door, and chasing him for a block down the Via Scalia until he vanished. He'd run in the direction of the Medici Palace, where he lived with Lord Lorenzo de'Medici, the wealthy patron of gifted artists.

She lumbered back down the Via Scalia toward the bakery, collapsing on the stone bench outside her shop. Her stomach was in flames. She rubbed her middle, chastising herself for letting Michelangelo once again get the better of her.

No more than five feet tall, his legs were sticks – the whole sack of him couldn't weigh more than a barrel of bread flour. Yellowish-brown eyes half hidden under sleepy lids were widely spaced. His plain hair was combed in stiff curls across his forehead. She had to admit that his looks were frightful, but she had a soft heart for Michelangelo – for all artists!

How she missed her Alessandro, whose chubby, winged putti flew up walls and over ceilings in churches throughout the city. But her son's talent was a mere raisin compared to the basket full of cherries that was Michelangelo's gift. And because she couldn't bring

110

herself to deny Michelangelo his favorite treats, she was doomed to die in Le Stinche.

Rising from the bench, she faltered a step, barely having the strength to open the bakery's creaky door. The scent of rosemary focaccia filled the shop. The woodsy smell from the ancient stone oven acted as a tonic and revived her.

Her granddaughter Celestina, who had smartly taken over business behind the counter, pleasantly winked at her. An invisible hot poker stabbed the inside of Simona's stomach.

Since Alessandro death, she was consumed with worry about leaving Celestina alone, with no inheritance. And now, if Simona were sent to Le Stinche, her granddaughter would have no one to protect her from the nighttime roving gangs of Reform Boys, who made it their business to burn up the city.

She ambled to the back room to catch her breath and calm her fiery stomach so she could return to work at full-strength and assist Celestina with their customers. To relax, Simona dug through the bag of cornmeal slouched in the corner where she hid a sketchbook of male nudes that Michelangelo had mistakenly left at the bakery a year ago, or thereabouts.

Digging through the yellow grain, she drew out the sketchbook, and then rested her sorry bones atop a small stool. With reverence she laid the book on her lap, and then with the back of her hand cleared traces of cornmeal sticking to its cover. She turned to the first page.

Portraits of young men with straight Roman noses, thick curling locks, and necks strong as tree trunks floated in the corners of action-packed pages. Their muscular torsos twisted, hard arms hoisted swords, and bulging thighs wrapped around the backs of wild-eyed horses. The lips Michelangelo drew on them were fleshy, so alive, that even at her age she was nearly seduced to kiss the images.

Flipping page after page, Simona was almost able to hear the grunt of charcoal-sketched stonecutters, their backs flexed under the strain of heaving rocks. She could nearly smell their briny sweat.

And front-sides were everywhere, without a single fig leaf for covering.

At night, recalling the pictures, she had to rub her own front side to release the hot longing. She bit back a pleased smile. She wasn't dead yet.

When the front door moaned open, she shoved Michelangelo's sketchbook back in the cornmeal. Celestina walked in, appearing none the wiser.

"Taxman Nerezza has come calling, again." Celestina's voice was just above a whisper.

Simona's knee buckled as she slid off the stool.

Celestina caught her by the elbow. "Are you sick, grandmother?"

Simona waved off her granddaughter's concern.

She saw the worry in Celestina's eyes when her granddaughter said, "I'll stand by your side."

Simona took Celestina's soft hand. "You've always been brave, but today I need you to stay here and knead the dough."

Stomach shaking like a thief at his hanging, Simona straightened her shoulders for Celestina's benefit and then sauntered out to face the taxman.

When she caught him throwing a pistachio cookie in his mouth, her stomach erupted like Mount Vesuvius.

He looked like the devil with his black hair growing in a peak down his forehead. Then, with no visible shame, he had the nerve to pick up another biscotti, and bit down. When it snapped, Simona's shoulders jerked.

He smirked. "Add two biscotti to that little fig Michelangelo's bill."

She swallowed her anger. The one person she knew not to pick a fight with was Nerezza, not today anyway. "Can I get you anything else?"

"Ten scudi."

Hands shaking, she fumbled inside the brown leather purse she kept tied at her waist. She dropped four scudi in his pale hand.

He looked at the coins belittlingly, as if she had paid in flour slugs. "Where's the other six?"

She swallowed hard. "I'll have them tomorrow."

"And how do you expect to raise that kind of money in that short a time?"

Simona rubbed the back of her neck. She had no idea. "I have an idea."

"All right Signora. You have until tomorrow, or pack for Le Stinche." His black cape flapped as he turned on his heel and out the door.

Simona collapsed to her knees. She was going to lose the bakery. Celestina would be left abandoned with neither dowry, nor inheritance. And it was because of that damned Michelangelo and the money he owed her.

Grabbing onto the counter, she steadied herself up. The thought of Celestina cold and cowering outside against a building in the dead black of night was too much to bear. Simona was getting her money today.

She threw a black veil over her hair, calling to Celestina. "I'm leaving for the Medici Palace."

"But grandmother – "

Simona didn't pause to answer. She tore down the busy Via Scalia, plowing through anyone who dared step in her way, and then rounded the corner to Via Cavour, where the Medici's lived. A tall, iron fence surrounded the grounds. She rattled the gate, catching the ear of a heavy-faced watchman dressed in Medici yellow, red, and blue stripes.

"I demand to see the face of Lord Lorenzo de'Medici," she said.

The guard gave a salacious grin. "And I demand to see le tette of Aphrodite, but that's not going to happen in our lifetime, either." He pretended to pinch his nipple.

Simona pursed her lips. "Get me your superior."

He swung his club. "I'm capo."

Bitter juices swirled inside her stomach. To get past the gate, she'd have to suffer a blow to her head.

From down the fence, a young, curly-haired blond watchman rushed to the gate. "Capo Bruno. Aspetta. Wait. I know who that is." Capo Bruno leaned in and the young guard whispered. Simona frowned. How did the young guard know her?

Staring at her through the iron bars, Bruno's eyebrows leapt in what appeared to be delight. An apologetic smile crossed his moustache-covered lips. "Welcome to Palazzo Medici Riccardi, Signora Judita," he said, jiggling his skeleton key in the gate's heavy lock.

Simona bit her tongue. She knew a Judita. Judita was once as beautiful as Venus, but no more. A customer mentioned that Judita died from a burst of fever only a few days back. But if Capo and the young guard thought she was Judita, she would comply. Simona was willing to be Joan of Arc if it got her inside the palace to speak to Lord Medici.

Capo heaved open the heavy gate. Simona slipped in swiftly. He nodded toward the young guard. "Follow Watchman DeMarco to the laundry. Lord Medici will see you after you've dressed."

Simona pulled her veil close, slippers moving with haste to follow the guard across the colonnade courtyard's soft, green grass. She wished her bubbling stomach would settle, but like her, it didn't know what to expect next.

With a brass key the size of his hand, the watchman unlocked the arched wood door leading into the palace's bustling red kitchen. Simona inhaled the pleasing scent of thyme and roasting meat.

She followed at DeMarco's heels down a narrow staircase into the laundry, a long, stuffy, colorless room in the bowels of the palace. An army of sweating women fixed hems, tended tears, and wrung out tunics.

"Head Laundress," snapped DeMarco. "Dress Signora Judita in the scarlet gown worn by Lady Nannina in her portrait."

Simona tugged DeMarco's sleeve. "Do you mind telling me –"

The head laundress, a sprite of a woman about her age or thereabouts, had Simona stripped and her waist cinched in a corset before Simona finished asking her question. Simona grimaced, blinking back tears. Her poor stomach was bound too tight in the girdle. Another laundress seized Simona's arms and hoisted them straight up. Yet another slipped a soft, red velvet dress over Simona's head.

Hands of every size were upon her, buttoning, straightening, and yanking. Simona's head spun.

Finished, the platoon of laundresses circled her, chattering in admiration of their work. One pretty girl, around the age of Celestina, remarked, "Lady Nannina never looked pretty in that dress. Signora Judita wears in like a queen."

The head laundress slapped the poor girl across the cheek. The other laundresses fell silent as the crack echoed around the windowless room. Simona sought an answer to what she was doing in Nannina's dress, but she shut her mouth tight, leery of the head laundress's ready hand.

"Lord Medici is in the biblioteca." DeMarco took Simona by the elbow, thankfully pulling her from the laundry.

Dashing down the long hallway to the library, she struggled to catch her breath under the weight of the gown.

DeMarco stepped aside and Simona crossed the threshold into the library. The richness of the room stole her breath a second time. Taking delicate steps inside, her head swiveled this way and that. Her eyes tried to count the volumes of gold-and-red-bound books, but there had to be a thousand lining the dark wood shelves.

When a small swath of books appeared to move, she clutched her chest. Blinking deliberately at the walking figure, she finally determined it wasn't the books that strolled, but Lord Medici himself, dressed in a gold tunic, white tights, and red slouching cap, the same colors as his books.

As he neared, she noticed one dark eye looked directly at her face, and other stared at the wall. His nose was long and thin, the tip pointing downward. His black hair was cut at his jaw.

Heart racing, she bowed her head and curtsied.

His smile was patient. "Signora Judita, you've changed since we last met. You are more beautiful than I remembered, and look nothing like my sister Nannina, which I suppose is a compliment to you."

She feared if she admitted she wasn't Judita he'd have her thrown out on her culo before she could ask for Michelangelo's debt to be paid. But for the compliment on her looks, she supposed she should thank him. "Grazie, my Lord. May I ask what I'm doing here?"

"Allow me to explain. I've commissioned one of my artists to paint a portrait of my sister, Lady Nannina de'Medici. He is finished with all but her face." He tugged at his collar. "I love my sister but she looks like a monkey."

Simona recoiled. "Poor woman!"

"I'm afraid it's true. You will be her face-double, and earn five scudi for your time. Now report to the studio."

Simona leaned back, frowning. Five scudi was too little an amount for the taxman, and she had no idea what he was talking about. Face double? "Scusi, Lord?"

"What's not to understand? You will sit still and my artist will paint your face instead of my sister's. Now run along." He waved his hand dismissively.

Simona's stomach flipped. She hadn't time for rich people games. Lunch customers were due any moment at the bakery, and she must not leave Celestina alone with all the work.

Simona thrust out her chest. "Thank you for the offer, Lord, but I cannot accept your two-face business."

His cheeks flushed the color of Nannina's dress. "So why are you here then?"

Simona cleared her throat. "To seek payment for the appetite of one of your artists. Michelangelo owes me six scudi – more with interest. Per favore, please, pay his debt and I shall be off."

His silence was like a knife that twisted through her belly button straight into her stomach. Tapping his finger on his chin, he sauntered to his bookcase, pulled out a book that was really a box, opened it, and extracted a purple velvet purse jangling with coins.

"If you sit for the portrait, I will pay you twice Michelangelo's debt."

"But I can't … the bakery."

Lord Medici fished six scudi from the purse. He approached her, coming close enough so she could smell the lavender oil he bathed in. When he tugged the bosom of her dress her blood turned cold. One by one he slid six coins down her bare cleavage, her chest rising up and down with each frightened breath.

"You'll earn the rest when the portrait is complete," he said.

She raised her trembling hand to her chest, to protect the precious coins. "I will accept these six coins as payment for Michelangelo's biscotti. But no more."

The Lord shrugged. "Watchman, take her to the basement and forget about her for a while."

She gasped, quickly grabbing Lord Medici's hand and shaking it. She had no choice. She could not wither in the Medici's dungeon. Celestina would be frightened and the taxman had to be paid. "I will sit for your ugly sister."

"Molto bene," said Lord Medici. "Very good. Now, watchman, escort Signora Judita to the studio."

Nannina's dress was heavy as chains as she ran to keep up with DeMarco's long stride. The pungent odor of charcoal and paint told her she was close to the studio.

Following DeMarco inside, she had to shade her eyes from the brilliant light. The walls and ceiling were made entirely of glass windows, and the mammoth rectangular room was noisy with much ringing and clamoring. Rows of young artists, barely old enough to shave, sketched important people with lye-lightened hair, pale faces, and the gift of being able to sit perfectly still. Others drew pictures of ripened apples and bronze pears in ceramic bowls.

DeMarco pointed to the far corner to an artist whose face was hidden behind his canvas. "You go with him."

Hauling up her heavy skirt, she passed Raphael, an artist who came into the bakery regularly. And paid his bill. Raphael's disposition was sunny as the studio he worked inside. His hazel eyes twinkled and his lips were stuck in a perpetual smile. He wore a gray and black slouchy hat high on his forehead over light brown, wavy hair. Simona sighed. If only she was a few years younger.

"Bon giorno Signora Simona, what brings you to the studio?" Raphael's tone was pleasant and welcoming.

She whispered in his ear. "I'm going to be the face of Nannina."

"Aha … si, si, si. Yes." He nodded knowingly. "Who's the artist?"

DeMarco pointed to the corner. Raphael looked worried. When she spotted him, her stomach lurched.

The artist glanced up from his canvas. "Mio e Dio," he snarled. "My God, it's you."

"Ciao, Michelangelo," she said flatly, stepping forward to peek around the canvas.

Michelangelo blocked her view. "No one sets eyes on my painting until I say."

She snorted. The son-of-bitch was even cheap when it came to giving a look at his work. She curtsied mockingly. "Yes, Lord Buonarroti."

He grunted, pointing at a high stool with peeling white paint. She heaved herself and the damned dress up. Taking her chin in his paint-speckled hand, Michelangelo directed her face toward the south wall. He grabbed her around the hips and yanked north.

Sitting with perfect stillness, sweat dripped between her breasts. She prayed the scudi would not slip out.

When a young assistant for Michelangelo turned the hourglass for the third time, Simona stretched her neck to release the tightness.

"Be still," Michelangelo snapped.

"I need to rest for a moment."

"Don't move," he warned. "And do not look and my work."

Through clenched teeth, she said, "I cannot stay this way a heartbeat longer."

He wiped his hands on a rag. "When I return, if I deem that your position has changed one hair, I will see to it that you receive no payment." Michelangelo then turned on his heel and stormed out of the studio.

Simona would have doubled over in stomach pain, but the damned corset kept her stiff as a dead goat. How dare Michelangelo threaten her with more no scudi. She could allow him no more leniencies.

Michelangelo must be shown she was not his slave. She whistled low for Raphael, who was cleaning his work area. "Do you want to make Michelangelo mad?" Her tone was conspiratorial.

Raphael smiled brightly.

"Let's look at his picture."

Raphael wagged his finger. "I've always liked you, Simona the Baker."

With comic flare, Raphael skulked around Michelangelo's easel. When he finally faced the portrait, he gasped. "Madre Mia! Mother of God, I can't believe what I'm seeing."

She couldn't tell if Raphael's reaction was good or bad, but as long as Michelangelo caught her and Raphael looking and became upset she'd be the winner.

Wiggling off the stool, Simona paused when Raphael spoke again. "He's turned Lord Medici's ugly sister into you, and yet it still looks like Nannina. And she's beautiful." He sounded thunderstruck.

She hurried around. And then all the noise and the stinking odors filling the studio fell away. There was no one else in the room but her and Michelangelo's painting. She inched in closer to examine the details. The setting was not the studio. It was the library with its rich red and gold army of books. She glanced down at the scarlet dress on her body. Michelangelo replicated it with precision in the painting, except the red was more vibrant, almost a living thing itself. The figure was seated in a high-backed chair that resembled a throne, and the body was bone slim and flat. All Nannina, no Simona.

When her eyes came to the face, her hand flew to her mouth. The face was hers, but so much more beautiful. Simona had been told often that she had pretty green eyes, but in the painting they were emeralds. Her skin was unlined, and her lips were full again and looked much like Celestina's. Simona had to swallow to keep the tears inside her eyes.

She had no idea Michelangelo saw her this way, more beautiful than she knew she was. He didn't just paint her face on a blank canvas; he gave her old face a young life.

She savored the image, but not for long. She barely had time to breathe before Raphael blanched at the sight of Michelangelo at the far end of the studio.

"You son of a whore Raphael. I told you not to look!" shouted Michelangelo, charging Raphael.

Michelangelo threw the first fist. And then Raphael wrestled Michelangelo to the ground. Raphael's easel toppled. Michelangelo's wild foot kicked a hole in his neighbor's canvas. Raphael's errant arm swatted a paint pallet, and blue liquid went flying, splattering across a grouping of finished pictures.

The other artists, models, and watchmen flocked to the fight, some joining in, other's protecting the art.

And then, at that moment, it hit Simona like a lightning bolt. She knew how to get even with Michelangelo for the biscotti.

Simona grabbed Michelangelo's painting and ran for the door. With Michelangelo's picture before her face, she slipped down and out the tiled halls of the Medici

Palace, through the red kitchen, and out the arched door. Guards rushing to the studio stopped in stride when she passed, their eyes trained at the ground. It seemed no one dared to question why the Lady Nannina de'Medici, in her rich scarlet gown, was running across the outdoor colonnade courtyard, through the iron-gate, and onto the Via Cavour.

Simona rushed down the Via Scalia and dashed up the outdoor steps to her apartment. She slammed the door, locked it behind her, and fished the six scudi out of her bosom. She dropped them in a blue porcelain bowl for safekeeping to give to the taxman.

She wiggled out of Nannina's heavy dress and left it in a pile on the wood floor of her sitting room. And then with great care she set Michelangelo's portrait on the mantle above her stone fireplace.

She stretched her arms as wide as she could, and listened to every bone in her body crack. Then she flopped into her comfortable caned chair and treated her eyes to Michelangelo's portrait, the one that she would swear to authorities had been destroyed during the fracas between Michelangelo and Raphael.

Leaning back in her chair, Simona laughed with satisfaction. The one thing she studied, even more than baking, was the value of a piece of art. And with its revolutionary use of color and dimension, young Michelangelo's "Portrait of Nannina de'Medici" was priceless.

Simona rose, and pouring herself a cup of brown raisin wine, considered the plan for the following day. Before the golden sun cracked the dark sky, she'd unearth Michelangelo's sketchbook of nudes that she kept hidden in the sack of cornmeal at the bakery. With

Michelangelo's long-lost sketchbook under one arm and the "Portrait of Nannina de'Medici" under the other, she'd travel the back dirt roads up the mountain to the walled city of Pisa.

Alessandro once mentioned the Duke of Pisa brokered in fine art. And, being a scoundrel, he preferred stolen pieces, for which he paid less and resold to the Vatican for a handsome profit. She'd run straight to the duke's palace and introduce herself as Judita and make a deal.

She also knew Lord Medici wouldn't forget about his sister's portrait. He had to know that the technique used by Michelangelo in that painting would make it worth more than the Medici Palace one day, and he was shrewd enough to know the painting would be worth far less with his sister's plain face. But the Duke of Pisa would never admit to dealing in stolen goods, and Lord Medici would have to buy it back from the Vatican, at even double the price, if he could afford that.

She also knew Michelangelo, and that he walked around in a half-crazed state. He couldn't remember money for biscotti, or to inquire about his sketchbook of nude men. When Lord Medici demanded to know what happened to the piece, Michelangelo's answer would be as useful as his empty purse. He'd been simply too hotheaded that day to keep track of Nannina's portrait.

She wasn't worried about the guards either. The worst they could say is that they saw Lady Nannina running around the palace with a picture in her hands.

Simona sipped her wine. It warmed her stomach, which for the first time in forever felt more happy, calm … and rich. She breathed easy, knowing that if anyone were to be traced to the stolen art it would be Judita, God rest her soul. Her fears of Le Stinche were forever in the past. And Celestina, and the rest of Simona's great-granddaughters all the way down the line, would be set for inheritances, for the ages.

Simona patted her stomach softly and smiled, feeling powerful as the little warrior who slayed Goliath.

Annemarie Schiavi Pedersen's stories are a rare chance for readers to visit the Italian Renaissance, a time of great art and enlightenment, but also superstition. That passion creates a dangerous mix for her sensual and sometimes scandalous characters.

The historical romance she is currently working on takes place in late 15th-century Florence. When a fiery muse is accused of being a witch, she and a brave stonecutter risk all to defeat the powerful young inquisitor who comes between them.

Annemarie is an award-winning author, journalist, and editor. She has a hunch there's gladiator DNA swirling in her blood. Needless to say, things about Italy drive her imagination wild.

She lives in metro Detroit with her husband Brian, an automotive engineer. They are parents to Beth (married to Chase), Nick, and Christina. Also, a black-and-white Siberian husky named Vito.

Visit Annemarie's website:
annemarieschiavipedersen.wordpress.com

Ms. Button inspires more from her students than she imagined.

Freewheeling Free Association and the Theme Park Rangers of Death
By Phillip T. Stephens

Helena Button touched her silver-blonde hair, and tossed her feather boa over her shoulder. *Just like a white winged dove,* she sang to herself. Unfortunately, the sight of the class waiting inside the door brought her crashing back to earth.

In the parking lot she had counted the days to retirement, a prospect she never really thought about until last evening. Retirement, an almost impossible image to conjure, and practically pointless for an associate professor denied tenure years before. Especially one forced to pick up adjunct classes at the community college just to make ends meet thanks to expenses she incurred due to her loser ex-husband. (A husband who still owed her ten years of child support and never paid a day of alimony since leaving her for a flat chested TA who, in turn, left him for the Dean of Sociology.)

Only last night Diana Dilcox, her Dean and cherished friend (who protected her from six different Department Chairs with agendas that shifted as often as the wind), told her after six glasses of wine that she planned to retire a year from May. Which left Button dangling in the wind with thirty-five years in the University's service and no firewall (she believed that to be the new buzzword) to protect her.

Button practiced her Ujjayi breathing to unbind the knots in her heart chakras, then buzzed through the classroom door to face the heathen horde. Before she stepped across the door plate, her laptop case slipped from her shoulder to her left elbow, and her bag slid from her right elbow to her wrist. Her heel caught the door plate, and she barely caught the door jamb with her right hand at precisely the moment her case flipped forward on the strap and, not being secured properly, the laptop inched free from the lid.

Morris—the dumpy kid with long hair—the one who sat closest to the door—stumbled from his chair to grab it before it crashed to the floor. She recognized him because he only wore food t-shirts and ate peanut butter sandwiches in class, leaving a ring of crumbs on the table and floor for the janitor to clean. Button would have thanked him except for the sight of Regina and Cooper leaping from their chairs to snatch a piece of paper the other students passed around the table.

Cooper wadded it into a ball and hid it behind his back, morphing his face into an obsequious grin. "Good evening, Ms. Button."

Regina and Cooper, the class rich kids. He with skin tight jeans and her with skirts so short she need never worry about hiding her panty lines. Cooper failed to submit a single written word after three weeks of class. Button fully expected him to show up during finals week with his daddy's lawyers demanding an A for attendance alone.

Button left Morris holding her laptop and charged into the room, pointing at the culprits with her right hand, even though her bag tried to pull her wrist to the floor. "Show me that. What is it?" Thinking to herself, even as she shouted, *What the hell am I doing? Are we back in high school?*

"Nothing," Cooper said, and she might have dropped the matter, but he backhanded the paper wad to his stoner friend Charles who batted it back and forth between his hands like a hot coal.

Button never saw Cooper without Charles (probably Cooper's ready supply of weed and other party drugs). She thought Charles might hand the paper ball to her, except Bob, the wiry kid with the Jesus skin on his phone, who never failed to point out that women, Blacks, the President, immigrants and liberals would send the country to hell in the devil's hand-woven hand basket, snatched it from his trembling fingers and hid it under his leg.

Her foot didn't fit quite right in her boot, but Button hobbled to her place at the conference table, slammed her bags beside the overhead and leaned across the table. She opened her palm and said gently, "Play time's over. Just give it to me and let's start class." Bob kicked it under the table.

Poor Morris continued to stand by the door with her computer. Perhaps she should acknowledge him, but a firm commander quashed rebellion before the flames spread. She kneeled to look under the table, chiding herself for mixing her metaphors. However, clear thinking required action, not purity of prose

She saw no sign of the purloined paper. A different culprit had snatched it. She squatted on her toes and held herself level with the table, peering just above the surface to reconnoiter her young rebels. Sweat formed at her brow. Even at six-thirty in the evening, the coastal Texas sun hammered the classroom windows as though it meant to melt the glass and the students with it. Button hated these early-September days when the air conditioning buckled under the siege machines of heat.

No one moved. She checked Naomi, a Black student with her head shaved to her skull, dressed in sleeveless work shirts and steel-toed boots. She ripped off her sleeves to display her neck-to-wrist snake and dragon tattoos. No, Button thought, Naomi was too no-nonsense for this kind of game, but if she did play, she would never buckle under pressure.

Creepy Alex, the white trash wannabe with homeboy cap and baggy clothes (usually a zipper jacket and Old Navy sweat pants) leaned as far back in his chair as possible without sliding under the table. He held his arms fully extended, fingers wrapped around his iPad as though the keep away game escaped his attention entirely. His disinterest made Button suspect him most of all.

Alex questioned Button's every word and followed every move with hooded eyes. He sat in the center of the room next to Jennifer (her brightest student and the closest to a liberal—or at least feminist—in the class). He also sat directly across from Button's chair, as though waiting to catch her in an outrageous politically incorrect statement that he could carry in complaint to the Chair.

Yes, Button placed her bets on Alex, until she heard a giggle at the far end of the table. By the window. Marlene the hippie always sat by the window, probably so she could drift outside in a drug-induced dream state. Button rose to her feet, which at five three likely intimidated no one, and cast a laser glare in the girl's direction. Marlene tried to hide another giggle behind fingers decorated with tie-dyed nails.

Definitely Marlene.

"For Chris' sake," Regina said, and snatched the paper from Marlene's lap. She reached back to toss it but Button scrambled to the end of the table before she could release. Regina countermoved by stuffing the wad into her cleavage.

Button cleared her throat. Marlene jumped from her chair so she could pass. Button stuck her open palm in Regina's smug face. She could easily pick it up, it rose from her breasts like an advertising display, but Button knew the rules about personal contact with students. In fact, she felt certain she had crossed several lines already.

Morris still stood by the door holding her laptop. He always chose the seat by the door so he could bolt before any other students when she dismissed the class. Button presumed he regretted that choice now.

"Give me the paper."

"This isn't high school."

"Your behavior, not mine."

Regina's father distinguished himself from the hundreds of other Houston real estate developers by advertising on afternoon television driving a Cadillac with amply bosomed blondes holding martinis and Winchester rifles. She covered the paper with her hand as though swearing on the Bible, and said, "It's personal business."

"So personal you showed everyone else," Button said. "Hand it to me or I take it because it's clearly public property the way it's sticking out right now."

Casting Button glances that implied she wished she carried her own Winchester rifle, Regina pulled the paper from her bosom like a snot-covered tissue from a box and handed it over between her thumb and index nails.

Button took her seat beside the overhead and thanked Morris for saving her laptop. "You can bring it to me now," she told him. Then, as though the paper were no big deal, she made a production of hooking the laptop to the projector and arranging her notes while ignoring the wadded ball.

Despite her cool performance, the temperature rose. She thought back fondly to autumns at Michigan State and evening classes in Morell Hall with her mentor Diane Wakoski— with open windows and fresh breezes blowing across the grass and into the room.

She missed the diffused lighting as well. Not the harsh buzzing neon of Houston classrooms. Houston lighting clashed with the blistering rays of late day sunlight and washed the room to cast a yellow white pallor on student skin. The lighting made them look like zombies. Not zombies picking Button's brain for morsels of wisdom to carry into the world, but leaving her skull in the gutter like a cast-off potshard before shambling away, still suffering from misdirected hunger.

Button longed for her days as a student when teachers challenged her to think with real questions and demanded her best in response; not the current classrooms where she catered to students who considered her their employee. Who expected an A for regurgitating every word she said and sucking up after class.

Intro to Creative Writing my ass, she thought. More like Intro to Creative Cluelessness. The girls thought they were feminists because being "women" entitled them to free passes. The boys pounded on iPhones to score points killing pigs with birds.

With playtime over, the students tossed themselves around the conference table like debris after a storm. Most of the girls, at least trying to sit at attention, prepared to write down everything without thought to prove their due diligence. The boys either slumped in their chairs, feet extended under the table with phones at arm's length and thumbs dancing across the screens, or else faces slumped over their arms pretending to scan their screens but really minutes away from deep and uninterrupted stupor.

What happened to the students of her day? Students who couldn't wait for class to engage in the odyssey of creative exploration? Who sat prepared at the conference table a good five minutes before their professors stepped through the door? Who waited with their pens out and recorders arranged so they wouldn't miss a word? After evening classes, like this one, they followed their professors to local watering holes—even the lecherous drooling wolves who lured them there with less thought to dispensing wisdom than chasing skirts.

Button taught creative writing, but she aspired to unleash artistry and genius. She wrestled for three hours nightly to open these minds to the great writers and poets of the age. She knew they never learned to write by reading romance novels or watching Jet Li.

Virginia Woolf, Charlotte Perkins Gilman, Doris Lessing, Zora Neale Hurston, Kate Chopin, Sylvia Plath, Anne Sexton, Flannery O'Connor, Eudora Welty.

Sadly, her Chair suckled at the bosom of transactional analysis—the Sesame Street seventies pablum from which her professors weaned—Ken McCrory, classrooms in circles and free writing exercise after free writing exercise. A tradition the Chair insisted Button perpetuate and to which she finally capitulated. (First because she repeated herself constantly and even osmosis failed. These morons wrote down every word she said and they still couldn't remember a single thought she shared. And next because free writing allowed them to latch onto something—however insignificant—in their brains to write about.)

She decided to open the wadded paper. She fought back her gasp. A naughty picture of herself bending over, labelled, "Ms. Button's Bottom."

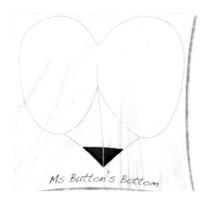

Ms Button's Bottom

She knew Alex drew it. He and his little iPad with its drawing apps. The only one not to take part in the keep away game. Nothing spoke to his guilt more loudly.

A strange one, that Alex, with his iPad and trade-paperback sized portable printer. In a modern University like Houston, students still complained when they couldn't turn in handwritten papers. He wirelessly printed in-class assignments.

Whenever she passed Alex, the lingering odor of Paco Rabanne followed, Paco Rabanne, the cologne to which teen boys graduated when they outgrew the ritualized male mating pheromone of Axe. It drifted from him in waves of feminine intolerance. How could Jennifer stand to be his friend? (Although, now that Button thought of it, Jennifer probably doused her own neck and shoulders with Barbie Mi during her turbulent high school years.)

The students waited for Button to react, suppressing giggles, thinking they got her goat with their little piece of erotica, if such an elevated description even applied. Little did they know how appropriately they timed their little gag to the lesson she had prepared for today.

She labored over today's exercise on Joyce and Molly Bloom, hoping to inspire them to transcend beer, bongs and butt tattoos. (And to stop the chair's accusations that she harped on women writers.) But now, well, she'd use the lesson to turn the tables. And maybe—just maybe—the passage about fellating a statue might set their little ears burning, if not lube a few gears in their sex-addled brains.

If nothing else the shock of discovering that sex and pornography preoccupied the general population generations before the Internet might prompt a scintillating paper or two.

Ms. Button's Bottom indeed. Let them see a real Button in Bloom.

"Joyce's passage explores the thoughts of Molly Bloom, who cuckolds her husband, the novel's protagonist, Leopold Bloom. The passage also projects Joyce's fears over the infidelity of his own wife Nora Barnacle, whom he horribly abused."

She broadcast Joyce and Nora's images from her laptop to the projector.

"Joyce refused to seek treatment for their mentally ill child. He moved Nora from their homeland Ireland to Paris and then left her at home while he drank away their income with his artist buddies. What woman wouldn't stray on him?" She flashed through images of Ezra Pound, Gertrude Stein and Sylvia Beach, whom she had no doubt they would never remember.

"In her youth she trysted with the actress Laura London* so the flow of fears in Joyce's own mind give rise to free association concerning Nora's infidelities." She flashed London's image on the screen, secretly proud of herself for having tracked one down on the Internet. In college she wrote a paper on their illicit relationship, a paper for which her professor—a man, of course—graded her harshly and accused her of making tenuous connections.

---

* *This is, in fact, a fabrication of Ms. Button's mind. There is no evidence that Barnacle and London engaged in anything beyond friendship.*

She read the passage where Molly dreams of fellating the statue. The girls scribbled even though they could read it on their own. The boys, well, she had no idea what the boys were doing. Were they looking it up on the Internet, or just surfing for porn? Alex held a stylus over his iPad, jotting, typing and scribbling. Occasionally he whispered to Jennifer, but she smiled and focused on her notes.

Button paused and waited for the class to come to attention. In her student days, a teacher's dramatic pause foretold the moment of an important announcement or revelation. Today's students took it as time to Tweet.

She'd fix that. "With this in mind, what does this passage stir in the recesses of your own brains?" she asked.

They stared at her with open expressions, half the boys not even aware she stopped speaking. The girls held their pens above their notebooks, wrists eager for permission to begin writing again. Alex, and it would be Alex, threw his shoulders back, crossed his arms—almost in a dare—and said, "It stirs the conjecture that we're doing another free writing exercise?"

Only Alex could not only take the wind from her sails, but shatter her midships like a cannon blast. Especially since she did, in fact, intend for them to free write about the Molly Bloom passage.

Fortunately, no one noticed the brief showdown.

As usual, the students wrote in a panic, their faces squeezed like oranges twisting into the juicer. The girls in a panic to avoid crippling brain freeze because their self-esteems denied them the ability to see themselves with academic futures. The boys' faces contorted in constipation, trying to squeeze out even one word like a single dingle clinging for dear life at the end of the wipe (admittedly a male metaphor but appropriate considering). Part of the stress stemmed from wrestling with pen and paper, since none of them was used to text outside of their smart phones. Most, no doubt, she attributed to the stress of tweaking the pitifully poor connections in the right sides of their art-starved brains.

Alex, however, scared her. With his determined smile he resembled nothing less than a serial killer stalking prey. His fingers danced across his virtual keypad faster and faster, his face illuminated by ungodly inspiration. Button's stomach turned at the thought of a young man so inspired by the image of a stone cherub penis.

The wall clock ticked off minute after minute, a surprising anachronism in a digital world. In the far corner of the room she heard the soft chirp of a game score from Manny who thought he had connected his ear buds.

She allowed thirty minutes. Only two managed more than a hundred words—Jennifer and Alex. Alex's printer hummed and hummed. And hummed. Twelve pages. She shuffled his to the bottom of the pile. If she read slowly, perhaps class might end before she read that far.

She started with Regina's. As expected, an anguished piece about a girl whose mother won't buy her a Porsche. Nothing at all to do with Molly or Leopold. She sighed. Now to stroke her egos. The first rule of millennial education: never disappoint. "Profound insights, Regina. You might have tied it into the passage in Ulysses a little bit more."

Naomi's. Trash talking the bitches at the Sharpstown Mall. Still no Molly or Leopold. "How inspired, Naomi. Perhaps if one of the bitches resembled Molly Bloom."

Marlene. A girl named Carlene loses it at a rave. Not at all biographical. "What depth of feeling, Marlene. Maybe Molly Bloom could have been thinking back on her night going to a rave."

Jennifer. A halfway decent piece about girlfriends hiding in plain sight. One of them wants to have sex with a boy who turns out to be a mannequin. Finally, a connection to the reading.

"Nice," she said. Unfortunately, department politics dictated you no longer held one student out in front of the others as the model to emulate lest you foster jealousy. "But somewhat vague. It needs more detail. We want to know who the girl is and why she dreams of this boy."

She made it through the girl's material. As much as she wanted to refer to them as "women." (It was, after all the mantra of her generation.) When a man referred to her classmates as "girls" they verbally castrated him. These creatures, however, remained light years of awareness beyond the brain power necessary to graduate to womanhood.

Button waded into the boy's assignments desperate to find anything nice to say about the inane drivel. Such as Bob's rant about a cop wrongly jailed for shooting an evil black kid. "The niger drawed on Brave Oficer Bob with too Heckler and Koch 45 compact tacticals. Bob only had his servis revolver and the manhood his father drilt intwo him from birth."

Don't even worry about the assignment, Button thought. "Bob, I can't help but wonder if Brave officer Bob isn't a projection of you. On the plus side, your spelling seems to have improved."

Charles' incomprehensible prose about smoking weed while watching the Simpsons left her completely baffled. In fact, the only parts she understood were "smoking weed" and "Homer Simpson."

"Charles, you really should work on your diction."

Charles ran his hands through his hair, speaking into the table at the same time. "But, like, you got the symbolism of Bart growing up to become Homer only to be Bloomed by his wife Marge cause he wouldn't share his primo Big Buddha, right?"

Button couldn't believe Charles articulated Joyce so well, even through the lens of his marijuana haze. Accident or coincidence? she wondered.

"You got all that from what Ms. Button read?" Naomi asked.

"Well, yeh? Didn't you?"

"Interpretation is subjective," Button said. "It takes years of training to read correctly." She almost failed to notice Naomi and Charles bumping phones to share numbers. She doubted they traded digits to set up a date.

Only Alex's paper remained. As much as she hated to admit it, she held the best example of writing submitted. He'd scribbled a last minute title on the first page: "Theme Park Rangers of Death."

She glanced at the clock. "Only twenty minutes left, and this looks rather long." As she expected, Cooper and Regina grabbed their backpacks to leave. Morris' chair was empty before she finished the sentence. Well, empty except for bread crumbs covered with peanut butter.

Jennifer raised her hand. "You could start at least." Cooper and Regina continued toward the door. Cooper flashed Jennifer a dirty look. Charles fumbled with his duffle bag, looking torn between Cooper and Jennifer's suggestion that they stay for the story.

"I kind a wanna hear the story," Charles finally said. "Alex writes like weed on speed." Cooper waved a fist at him, but Charles dropped the duffle between his feet and hooked his feet around his chair legs like anchors. Marlene leaned across the table to high five him.

Button thought she saw week-old weed smoke break free from their sleeves. Naomi flexed the snakes on her biceps. "I'd like to hear it too."

"I'll read as much as I can," Button agreed, trying her best to suppress a disappointed sigh. Cooper and Regina made no attempt to stifle theirs. Cooper stretched a sigh so dramatically he ruffled Regina's hair. Regina, in the meantime, dropped into Morris' seat. Cooper stomped back to his spot next to Charles.

Button cleared her throat. "Deep in the subterranean basement of the U of H Science and Engineering Research Building, Professor Leopold Bloom and his team conducted unauthorized research into velociraptor DNA. He knew it was forbidden but it came to him during a fevered dream when he was a lowly TA while his wife Molly carried on in the next room with his supervising professor Dr. Thomas Rex, a man known for his big head and tiny hands.

"The shameless Molly and lascivious Dr. Rex tormented Leopold night after night with their fellating and lovemaking, often leaving their dirty laundry tossed loosely around Leopold and Molly's tiny two-bedroom married student housing apartment, until Leopold made it his solemn vow to upstage Rex with a discovery so revolutionary it would forever devour his mentor's contributions to science.

"That night the incubator alarms rang—the eggs ready to hatch; the event horizon, if you will, consuming every previous event in his life. The first egg cracked and the tiny creature appeared, followed by another and then another. His team broke open the champagne and prepared to upload the videos.

"But the creatures continued to grow. The experiments dislodged the genetic inhibitors controlling aging. The raptors devoured Leopold, devoured his team assistant Leslie, and even devoured the unfaithful Molly who had continued to research at his side.

"Little did they know, the Theme Park Rangers of Death, who averted similar disaster in a major motion picture and three mediocre sequels, had stumbled across Leopold's plans during an Internet sweep and waited outside the lab in case disaster occurred. When the beasts burst through the building doors, they leaped into action. Three Jeep Rangers fully equipped with missile launchers, laser blasters and a team of five fully trained rangers with plasma rifles (action figures sold separately) scrambled from the parking lot to the lobby entrance.

"Col. Ron Alpha, team leader, gave the command and the team followed the raptors onto the green, firing three precisely timed missiles at the fleeing beasts. Unfortunately, Bloom blended shark and cheetah DNA into their matrix for speed and maneuverability and the missiles wandered past them into the frat boy SUVs illegally parked in handicapped spots.

"The laser blasters skipped past the raptors and into campus police cars answering the alarms about a major ruckus outside the science lab. 'Colonel Alpha,' breathlessly shouted Lt. Sara Sweetbottoms, his lusty but hardbodied second-in-command, 'these bastards are tougher than we thought.'

"They chased the raptors through the lot, into the main road, into faculty parking, across the main and into the Roy G. Cullen general classroom building where Helena Button held her creative writing class. The team abandoned their Rangers and pursued on foot."

End of page 7. The clock read 9:30. Saved by the bell. "Well, that's it for class tonight," Button said. "We'll pick this up Thursday."

"No way," Naomi said. "You just got to the good part."

Charles pumped his fist in the air. "This story rocks. You can't leave us hanging sis…I mean, Ms. Buttons."

Button glanced around the room. Even Cooper looked rooted to his chair. Against her better judgement, Button flipped to page 8.

"The creatures burst through Button's door and leaped onto the conference table tossing the scared students against the walls. Once in the confines of the tiny classroom, however, the beasts lost the room to maneuver. Sergeants Deeks and Dovers took the first two out with their plasma rifles, blasting them through the windows.

"The surviver, the alpha female, was a cunning bitch. She went straight for Ms. Button's throat, hoping to hold her hostage. Colonel Alpha took the corner and Sweetbottoms rolled under the table to take her out in a plasma crossfire before she could mutilate any more students. But at what cost? For the crossfire also quadrasected Ms. Button's body, leaving nothing standing but her Stevie Nicks boots and a blue wisp curling toward the ceiling in front of the board."

Even though four pages remained, Ms. Button lost her grip on the pages.

"I do not wear Stevie Nicks boots."

She couldn't believe that was her first reaction, and yet she still glanced down at her feet. Well…, maybe they could be seen that way, they were maroon suede. But that wasn't her intention. Although she wore out her Walkman playing "Stand Back" in college.

Get a grip on yourself, woman, she thought.

Every one of her students waited to see what she intended to do next. Not like students anticipated their college exams so much as deer walking into a clearing and discovering dozens of hunters with high-powered rifles aimed at them. "I see I finally have your attention," she said. Only when she said it, she felt like she morphed into the deer in the sites.

She tried, unsuccessfully, to catch her breath. And realized she inadvertently threw the gauntlet to that wiseacre Alex. And he drew first blood.

She also realized she wasn't thinking, she was speaking out loud. Even worse, that little uppity blonde Jennifer gripped Alex's shoulder as though declaring him the winner. Little post-modernist liberal Jennifer— postmodernist liberal meaning sell-out and see the "big picture."

"Ms. Button," Jennifer said, "I know you fought for women's rights, but there's so much more to women's rights than in your day. There's a bigger picture."

Button clutched her clavicle, choking on the tiny pocket of air remaining in her throat. The naive little know-it-all actually had the nerve to say those words?

"Bigger picture?"

The classroom fell silent as every student realized Jennifer ushered forth a never before spoken blasphemy. No one could articulate the nature of her blasphemy, but they knew she had blundered into one.

Cough. Pregnant Pause. Cough. "Is this what modern education's come to?" Ms. Button finally said. "Why, women have made no progress at all." Then the blood rushed her face like the charge of the last brigade.

She leaned across the table, even though Alex tried his best to look away. "It's your fault," she said. She grabbed his chin between her fingers, forcing him to face her. "It's all because of smiling smart-ass…" she put her free hand to her mouth, unable to believe he provoked her to use such language, "…so-called satirists like you."

She grabbed the papers, rolled them into a thick baton and briskly beat Alex about the head and shoulders.

Alex threw up his hands. "Ms. Button, it was an assignment."

But she didn't hear him over the roar in her brain. She smacked his hands, his shoulders, his neck, his chest.

"I didn't think. My mom says I'm too impulsive."

Jennifer put her hand on his shoulder. "Don't apologize. That's the old you. Be the new assertive you."

Button continued the thrashing even as she dressed Jennifer down. "And you, Ms. Transactional Analysis. This is writing, not Pop Psych 101."

"Hey, that was my writing. Not hers," Alex said. His voice lacked his usual combination of sarcasm and combativeness. Button knew she had finally established her position as the authority in the classroom. She battered his ears, the crown of his head, his fingers, his iPad, his nose.

Jennifer poked him again, this time in the back. "Stand up for yourself."

He sat straight. "Jennifer's right. This is creative writing, not Poly Sci 212 Mollifying Your Feminist Teacher."

Button dropped the papers and grabbed Alex's collar. She lifted him from his seat. One of his moronic male allies (naturally) threw up his phone to take video and then others followed his example, which only made her madder. Jennifer stuck her hand between them, the three of them tangled and before Button knew what happened, Alex's jacket unzipped from his neckline to his navel.

Jennifer dropped into her chair and apologized. Alex pushed his chair all the way to the wall, standing to escape the women's fury. Button lost her balance and collapsed to the floor, knocking her chin on the table, but still allowing her full sightline of the room. Alex's jacket fell open to reveal a tight sport's bra binding his breasts to her chest. Cooper leaped from his chair to the window sill shouting, "No fucking way."

Ms. Button scrambled against the molding but couldn't get her grip. Finally, Naomi grabbed her forearm and lifted her into her seat.

Jennifer grabbed the two halves of Alex's jacket and tried to reconnect the zipper but the zipper head clattered across the conference table and off the edge. Alex clutched the pieces below his breastbone and stared at the floor so he wouldn't have to face the class.

Bob rose from the table and announced, "I will not share a classroom with an abomination from the Lord."

He exited with his nose so high in the air he missed breaking it off on the door frame by inches.

"I told you there was a bigger picture," Jennifer said.

Ms. Button pointed her finger, which trembled so much she thought it might go into epileptic seizure on its own. "You're a woman?"

"I'm a man," Alex said.

"He's a man," Jennifer said simultaneously. "But biologically the state still treats him as a woman." She fumbled in her purse and found two safety pins. She helped Alex fasten his jacket to cover the bra. "Which is why I would think you, of all teachers, would be more sensitive."

Regina said, "Yeh, you being a feminist and all. You should be okay with his expressing his inner male." She crossed a pair of legs underneath a skirt that barely covered her hips when she stood. Then she reached into her backpack for her clutch and removed her makeup case.

Cooper slid back and forth against the window sill, his palms gripping the wood so tightly he could have pulled out the frames with a tighter squeeze. He muttered over and over, "No fucking way. He's a queer. He'll want to marry my sister. Or my brother. Or my sister. Or my brother."

Charles finally grabbed him by the elbow and slapped the side of his head. "Dude, you should be so lucky, the assholes your sister sleeps with."

Alex said, "I'm not gay, I'm a heterosexual male in a woman's body. And, yes, as a biological woman, I should be allowed to write and act like a male." He tried to force his zipper to catch but nothing happened. Then he slammed his fist on the table. "I'm still a feminist. And I don't treat women like shit the way you treat men, Ms. Button."

Button flattened her right palm to her chest. "I don't treat men badly."

The class chimed in unison, male and female.

"Could have fooled us."

"Yes, you do."

"Seems like it to me."

Jennifer raised her hand. "I have an idea for an assignment, Ms. Button."

Button gathered her class notes and stuffed them into her portfolio. "We've had enough writing today, Jennifer." She clicked the Windows shut down button on her laptop.

Jennifer ignored her. "Let's write a story about what happened today. You'll be the main character. We'll write how our characters really feel about your character."

Ms. Button opened her mouth to veto the suggestion but before her words emerged, the class agreed unanimously it was the best English assignment ever. She glanced at the papers which she still had to retrieve from the floor and realized she lost the energy to argue. All she wanted was a bath with her pink Himalayan crystal salts, a glass of Quivera Sauvignon Blanc and a pipe full of banana kush.

At least she had excited them about learning again.

Now she just had to explain to her chairman when he saw the videos on You Tube.

Phillip T. Stephens lives with a Hell's Granny and is proud to do so. She kicks his ass into shape daily, otherwise he would lounge in bed all day and watch alternating episodes of Fringe and the X-Files. Phillip and his wife Carol foster cats for austinsiameserescue.org and have successfully adopted more than 300 rescues in the last fifteen years. Twenty percent of the proceeds of his latest novel *Seeing Jesus* will be donated to rescue.

His other novels include *Cigerets, Guns & Beer, Raising Hell* and *The Worst Noel*.

@stephens_pt
ptstephens.com
gdimonday.com

Leo wants a peaceful life, but the resurrection of a 17th-century witch paints a different picture.

The Artist and the Crone
By Mark Cassell

I guess there will always be something in Mabley Holt to keep me here. Even after all the crazy stuff back in the spring, I returned and bought this tiny cottage with its equally tiny garden hemmed in by a precarious ragstone wall. As a man of little needs this was a perfect place to settle.

Perhaps it was stupid to think things wouldn't catch me up.

My one neighbour whose cottage was marginally larger than my own was a young lady of a similar age to me, with a reserved smile. If I thought my garden needed attention—those nettles were tall enough to sting your face—hers was equally neglected. We'd acknowledged each other when I'd moved in and that had been it.

After three weeks and kind of settled in, I dozed in front of a late night TV programme. A scream jerked me upright. On my feet, I staggered. That shrill cry still echoed, if not through the house but through my head. I yanked open the front door and stepped into the night. A cold moon pushed down on me just as the cold paving pressed up into the soles of my feet. I ran towards my neighbour's house. The place was silent and dark.

She'd had a nightmare, that was all. I headed back inside to bed.

Morning came and I awoke to the sound of thumps and clatters as though someone threw things in temper. I leapt from bed and raked fingers through my hair. Pulling aside the curtains without thought of my nakedness, I glared out the window and into her garden.

Dressed in a paint-spattered jumper and jeans, my neighbour stood beside a wheelie-bin. Its lid was up and rested against the ivy-shrouded fence. She was upending a number of shoeboxes and cartons, pouring out paint bottles and brushes and all manner of art supplies. Swiping away her dishevelled hair, she stepped backwards and looked up.

At me.

I twisted sideways, suddenly realising how naked I was, and the edge of the dresser stabbed my spine. She must've seen me. I waited, my back pressed to the cold wood. By the time I leaned sideways and peaked around the curtains, her garden was empty. She hadn't even put the bin lid down.

The day came and went; a day that I spent reading. Recently, I'd been reading a lot. All the books I'd inherited, books that truly belonged in a museum, were a mine of information that I hoped would help me understand a little piece of my troubled past. I'd even thumbed through a few books relating to local witch trials—it seemed Mabley Holt hadn't escaped witchcraft back in the 17th century, and given the small dealings I previously had with a magic that was most definitely black, that came as no surprise. The Shadow Fabric, a sentient darkness, was perhaps the most blackest of the arts imaginable.

Having just finished dinner, I heard my neighbour scream again. Only this time much closer, from outside perhaps. I took the stairs two at a time and ran into my bedroom, to the window. She stood in her garden, her face illuminated by the roaring flames from a twisted, shrunken bin. Thick smoke corkscrewed upwards.

Back downstairs again, I snatched my boots and yanked them on. One was bulkier now I'd modified it to conceal a weapon—these days I was always prepared. Keeping the Witchblade to hand was comforting, and as far as I could tell it was the only one in existence. I yanked open the back gate and ran alongside her house, over cracked paving and brambles threatening to trip me. The crackle of flames was louder as I approached. I stumbled into her garden. The stink of plastic and chemicals stung my nostrils.

Dressed in the same paint-splashed jumper as when I'd seen her that morning, she threw me a glance then looked back at the fire. Flames roared. Spirals of grey-black smoke reached the twilight clouds.

She scanned her garden. I guessed she looked for something to put out the fire. If we could contain it fast enough we'd not need the fire brigade. I ran over to where a hose coiled, tangled with grass.

"This attached to anything?" I shouted.

She nodded, hair catching in her mouth. She hooked it out.

"Turn it on!"

She seemed doubtful for a moment. I dragged the hose closer to the flames as she vanished round the corner. Heat prickled my face. The hose jerked, spat, then hissed a stream of water and I directed the nozzle around the edge of the inferno. Smoke belched and I cupped a hand over my mouth and nose. Waving the hose left and right, I doused the flames and gradually worked inwards. Defiant at first, the fire diminished.

Eventually, I stood back but kept the hose aimed at the dirty rainbow of molten colours. Several fence panels showed a few scorch marks. The ivy had burnt away and water dripped from the shrivelled and blackened ends.

"Reckon you can turn it off now," I said.

Her face, although relieved, seemed to shrink. Her mouth slightly open, she disappeared round the corner again. I heard a couple of squeaks and finally the flow dribbled. She returned just as the last drip splashed my boot.

"I'm Leo," I said.

"Pippa," she whispered, "and thank you."

I coiled the hose in a pathetic attempt at neatness, and dropped it on a rusted garden chair. My cuff had ridden halfway up my forearm and something made me quickly tug it down to hide the mark, the scar—I've called it a scar all along but I've always known it was more than that.

For something to say, I said, "Guess you're an artist."

"I wish I wasn't."

"That why you threw all that stuff out?"

"Yep." Tears welled in her eyes and she glanced away, wiping them.

"Flammable, that stuff."

She held one hand in the other, squeezing her thumb. "Thank you."

"You've already said that."

A weak smile pushed into her moist cheeks.

"W—" I began.

Something crashed from inside her house. It sounded like deckchairs collapsing all at once.

"Not again!" Pippa yelled and ran indoors.

I followed, unable to work out whether I'd seen fear or anger in her face.

We entered the kitchen first. The aroma of fresh coffee overwhelmed me. Plates and cutlery were stacked high in a sink filled with filthy water, and a scatter of cornflakes covered the counter. Into the hallway next. The layout was similar to my own and where my back room had become a library, she'd converted hers into a studio. Or at least it seemed her intention; the carpet was half rolled across the room to reveal the floorboards.

Pippa flicked the light switch but nothing happened. Desperation made her try again. And again. On, off. On, off. Click. Click. Click…

"Stop it," I told her.

The final click echoed and fell into the silence.

Evidently this was where the noise had come from.

A shrinking evening light cast a blue haze into the room. Five canvasses of varying sizes were strewn across the bare floorboards in the jagged clutches of splintered easels. Paint of all colours had soaked into the pile and peppered the floorboards. Bottles and brushes were all over the place. The black was still spreading, flowing between floorboards.

Pippa's hands twisted together. "I've so many deadlines approaching."

I didn't know what to say.

"And then all this crap happens." She squeezed tight her eyelids. "I can't handle this."

She had skill, yet the content was questionable. One painting depicted a landscape; hills and fields and a brooding sky. In the foreground an oak tree loomed over the bodies of men, their tunics clawed open around red and ragged wounds. The way some of those men held themselves suggested not all were dead. Blood soaked the grass. From a gnarled branch above dangled a woman dressed in rags, her neck broken and hooked in a noose. Such was the detail you could hear the men groan, the rope creak, and almost see the woman's body swing.

Another was of a village market square. A crowd gathered around a pyre, its flames licking the night. At its heart, thrashed an elderly woman tied to a wooden post. In the shadows at the rear of the crowd, several men writhed on the uneven paving, their faces a bloody mess. Again, such was Pippa's skill I heard the crackling flames, the woman's screams.

The other paintings depicted similar scenes of women dying; drowned, stabbed, beheaded. The latter was particularly gruesome.

I had no doubt as to who or what these women were: witches. After all that happened to me at the beginning of the year, was I again dealing with witches?

"Please don't judge me." Pippa's voice drifted over my shoulder.

I pushed fingers through my hair. It was getting long and I realised I hadn't had it cut for over a year.

"I know what you're thinking," she continued, "but I don't usually paint this kind of shit."

"You have no idea what I'm thinking."

She picked red paint from her cuff.

"Let's put it this way," I added, " I have books that delve into the history of witchcraft. I'm talking about a real history you won't find anywhere in your local library. Or online."

She crouched and pulled a canvas towards her. It was the one of a woman's limp body being dragged up a riverbank by whom I suspected to be the Witchfinder General himself—a man who in the 17th century unceremoniously tortured women suspected of witchcraft. He was beneath the shadowy arc of a bridge. The darkness that clutched the stonework churned as though sentient, its coiled tendrils extending towards the cheering men above.

Together, Pippa and I propped the canvasses against the wall and set aside the splintered easels. Her work really was good. There was something about the way she used subtle brush strokes around the figures that gave the impression of motion. There must be a technical term for it but I wasn't an art critic. She had talent, that much was obvious.

Then I found a sixth canvas, smaller than the others. My hands froze.

"What is it?" Her voice was tiny.

I stared at the painting. Of all of them, this one was unfinished—or at least appeared to be. It was a landscape focused around a wall of looming rock, moss-covered and ancient. In their shadowy embrace, dark clumps of what appeared to be fungus covered the leaf-strewn ground. But on the rock, the symbol—the *sigil*, as I'd recently learned—was barely noticeable yet it was there like some prehistoric cave painting. Faded red, a symbol of two triangles facing one another, one hollow, the other solid, and separated by a crude X.

"Leo?"

I touched my sleeve—an unconscious habit now. I should've known this would never end.

I relaxed my jaw. "These are good."

"What is it?" She demanded, her voice now even smaller.

"I…"

"You recognise it." Her chin quivered. "That symbol."

"Yes."

"What does it mean?"

"Pippa, I—"

Behind us, the floorboards creaked.

Timber groaned and split and heaved as though something pushed from beneath. Nails pinged around us. Pippa shrieked and ducked, and something stung my cheek. From between splitting planks, a cluster of shadows bubbled. Like liquid it oozed upwards and stretched as though testing the air. Faint strands coiled and whipped, spraying flecks of darkness like black tentacles flicking ink.

"What's happening?" Pippa shouted.

From my boot, I pulled out the Witchblade.

She stumbled backwards, wide eyed. She stared at the spreading darkness—those sentient shadows I was all-too-familiar with—and then back to the curved blade in my hand. "Leo?"

I stood between her and the shadows, pointing the blade towards the expanding darkness. Already the tip spat white energy. That ozone smell—something I'd almost forgotten—teased my senses, somehow comforting. This reassurance of its power was short-lived however, as the oppression of the shadows constricted not only the light but peace of mind, sanity, anything *positive*. It made me want to turn the blade on myself, to push its length through my jacket, to feel my intestines slice open... The warmth, the freedom...

I shook my head. "No!"

Pippa shuddered. By the look on her face she was having equally disturbing thoughts. She glared at me.

The shadows thickened and a thin tendril shot towards us, towards me. It snatched the Witchblade from my hand. I grabbed air as the shadow snaked back into the growing nest of darkness.

"That was not supposed to happen," I said. There'd been a time when the shadows were afraid of the damn thing.

Pippa had pushed herself against a far wall. "None of this is supposed to happen."

As though holding their breath, the shadows sucked inward and released the weapon. With a glint of fading daylight, the blade thumped an angled floorboard. It spun, then slid and came to rest on one of the straighter, untouched boards.

I started forward, reaching out.

"Don't!" Pippa screamed.

The Witchblade twitched and jumped and landed again with a clunk. As though an invisible hand grabbed it, the blade stabbed the timber...then scraped along the grain. Wood curled in its wake, nearing the spilled black paint.

My lungs tightened. All the books I'd read since the chaos at Periwick House, the sentient darkness of the Shadow Fabric, the reanimated dead, the deaths of those I'd known…all I'd learned during and after that time, was useless. These shadows were different. Sentient as before, but this was something else. And when the blade—my Witchblade—dipped into the paint and began to write, I knew this was entirely something else.

H…

"What the—?" I shouted.

H…E…

Pippa pushed herself against me, tugging my jacket.

HELP.

What the hell was going on?

ME.

"Leo?" Pippa whispered.

The blade clanked to the floor, spun once, and was still.

HELP ME.

The heaviness in the room somehow weakened, my brain clearing. Whatever supernatural Being was behind this had apparently spent its energy. The darkness had fully retreated, to bubble like a pool beneath the split floorboards. It seethed, spitting shadows like puffs of smoke.

I stepped forward and pulled Pippa with me—she still had my jacket in her hands.

"Um, sorry." She let go and straightened, seeming taller. She was still about a foot shorter than me.

Spreading my stance, I grabbed the Witchblade. Nothing happened.

She eyed the weapon.

"Let's get out of here." I told her. I didn't know what else to say, what else to do. This was her home certainly, but what could we do? And who the hell had written that message?

Once again the floorboards creaked and heaved, though not as fierce as before. Rusted nails screeched. The darkness oozed from beneath and streaked across the wood, stretched over the skirting and up the wall. It spread like damp blemishes, only thick and black.

I nudged Pippa towards the doorway. "Go!"

The door slammed just before we reached it.

Pippa actually laughed. "Of course."

More darkness blossomed. We backed up. The window was our only exit. I glanced around for something heavy enough to smash it. I went to grab an easel, and...

In a surge of shadow and brick and mortar, a portion of wall burst outwards into the garden. Twilight and cold air rushed in. Brick dust swirled. Dry, bitter.

I looked back at the door. The darkness spread across the wall and over the door panel, the knob vanishing in a twist of shadow. Whether this was a supernatural entity or even the Shadow Fabric, it seemed we had only one exit. I left the easel where it was.

"Go!" I shoved her towards the heaped masonry. "Now!"

She staggered and I gripped her shoulder, steadying her. My neck tingled, feeling the encroaching darkness. Rubble shifted beneath our feet and we made it into the garden. The Witchblade was still in my hand yet there was no energy coming from it. Cold and useless.

I had no idea where to go.

Further ahead, separating our gardens, the ragstone wall exploded. Dust and darkness bloomed, the grass heaved. Deep-rooted shadows churned in the crumbled remains. I'd seen this before, back when I'd witnessed the Shadow Fabric burst from the ground. Yet this was different, *everything* that was happening was different.

At some point I'd grabbed Pippa's hand. She was cold. For a moment I thought of heading for my house but that was absurd; there'd be no safety so close.

From the edges of uprooted ground, like some kind of black fungus, dark streaks broke across the grass, curling and bursting and mixing with the earth. Sweaty, glistening heads bulged and split, oozing black goo and bleeding into the shadows.

This was most definitely different than anything else I'd experienced.

Pippa's hand wrenched from my grip and I staggered. She was no longer there.

I scanned the collected shadows, natural or otherwise. More of that fungus smothered the grass and weeds, choking foliage.

Her cry echoed from somewhere ahead. I stepped sideways, forward and back. Where the hell—

Beyond the crumbled wall, along the row of trees that marked the surrounding fields, a cluster of shadow thickened. Beneath over-hanging branches, Pippa's face, pale and wide eyed, stared back at me.

Her muffled cry of "Leo!" echoed as though even further away.

I leapt over the sprouting fungus. How had she travelled so far? I sprinted. Almost there, and…her body stretched with the darkness, her form rotating, churning like curdled milk. She vanished. Only to appear again further away, past the trees and in the fields. More fungus spread, and again she cried out.

I charged towards her, my arms pumping close to my body, my feet slamming hard on the uneven ground. The Witchblade spat weak pulses of energy, somehow depleted. Having been touched by the shadows, perhaps its power had been drained. I had no time to think on it.

Again in a blur of black and white her image phased into an almost ghost-like streak. Then vanished. Still I ran. How many more times will she vanish and reappear? Finally to be lost altogether? Tall grass whipped my legs. Up ahead, the sweaty heads of fungus glistened in the fading light as if to guide my way.

Pippa's silhouette ricocheted from tree to tree, merging with the shadows. Shimmering images of her leapt from shadow to shadow, across fields, appearing and disappearing. Again and again... Her screams were muted; a constant echo.

Still, I ran.

Up a gradual rise, her image flashed yet again. It clung to the natural shadows between trees. Faint at first, then her terrified face sharpened, bright in contrast to the seething darkness that trapped her.

"Help me!"

Her words reminded me of the message written in her studio. Was that Pippa who now screamed it or was it whoever had used the Witchblade to write in the paint?

She vanished.

My breath short, I made it to the tree line. More fungus ate into the foliage to mark the way. I kept the trees to my left and charged past. Into another field. Up ahead, a jagged outline cut the deep blue of twilight sky. Once a barn or some kind of outhouse, crumbled walls hid in a sea of nettles and tangled brambles. A corrugated roof, rusted and buckled, lay beneath heaped bricks and rotten timber. The fungus, the thickened shadows, ended.

There was Pippa. But—

No, it couldn't be her.

Wisps of shadow drifted over the brickwork, blending with a dozen images of her sitting on the ruined walls.

Closer, and I saw it wasn't Pippa but several different women dressed in rags or long skirts, filthy and sodden. A storm of shadow obscured their heads, hiding their faces. One had a noose around her neck while another sat cradling her arm. Another held a bundle of rags close to her bosom, perhaps a child. One of the women, whose hair dripped a liquid darkness, kicked at a black mess at her feet.

My pace slowed. I had no doubt these women were witches. Whether practitioners of black or white witchcraft, they were here. *Ghosts* of witches, and Pippa had painted their deaths.

I jogged to a halt.

As if to acknowledge me, their limbs jerked. Excited almost. Their heads swayed with the darkness that hid their faces. Wisps of shadow skittered around them, teasing. In turn, the darkness fell from their heads. Faceless. Framed by unkempt hair, their smooth and mottled flesh stretched blank where faces should be. Stretched like a canvas. Dark veins bulged ready to burst from the skin. One had her hair tied back in a red scarf, though most left it straggly and knotted. Others kept it long. But their faces. Holy shit, their faces. Or lack of.

I tightened my grip on the Witchblade and approached.

Fungus crawled up the brickwork, teasing the mortar. The black vines brushed one of the women's dangling bare feet.

As I neared the ruin, I saw Pippa. Finally.

Across an expanse of swaying nettles, Pippa slumped against crumbled brickwork. Of all the women here, she was the only one whose image was sharp, clear. She hunched in shadows that appeared to boil from the ground, her arms outstretched and bound by loops of darkness. It was like she was crucified.

I rushed forward and tripped. My knees thumped the ground.

Around me, a deepening darkness twisted and uprooted clumps of earth. Vines as thick as my forearm snaked upwards, daring me to approach further. The trunks split and black spores puffed, clouding the air.

I held my breath and scrambled up. There was no way I wanted to inhale that crap. I backed off. Shadows thickened, blackening the grass and spreading further to the left and right. More vines twisted with the earth, their lengths splitting open with tiny mouths dribbling fungus and spores. Barbs pushed from beneath grey flesh, curved and wicked.

A wall of shadow swept up, blocking my advance.

I thrust with the Witchblade. The blade sliced through the darkness and when I yanked it out, the jagged tear sucked closed again. There was no Witchblade fire, no power or strength to be gained when brandishing it; I may as well have been holding a dinner knife.

I took another step back as those vines slithered towards me. Those barbs looked nasty. Spore clouds drifted.

"Why the hell did you lead me here?" I yelled beneath my hand as I clamped it around my nose and mouth.

A torrent of shadow roared above the ruined walls, blending with the onset of night, obscuring a moon desperate to break through the clouds. Amid the roiling darkness, images flickered like TV screens. Each showed another place, another time.

"What is this?" I demanded.

...A swinging noose from an oak tree...

"Tell me!"

...Deep water and flailing limbs...

Pippa's scream echoed, muted in the darkness. "Leo!"

...Blood pouring from wounds along a slender arm pricked with needles and sliced with daggers...

Memories. Each mirrored Pippa's paintings to reveal the suffering and individual deaths of these women. Perhaps they were innocent of witchcraft or were even white witches, never using their craft for the dark arts.

As one, these phantoms raised an arm. Clumps of shadow and filth dripped from sleeves. They pointed at Pippa.

Still I couldn't advance, couldn't help her. She struggled in the embrace of a thickening darkness, stitched into the shadows. She writhed, jerking her head back and forth. "Leo!"

Beneath her the ground bulged.

I lunged forward and smaller vines whipped up. A billowing cloud of spores filled the air. And again, I backed off.

The ground shook and through the tangle of nettles near Pippa's kicking feet, a barbed trunk as thick as a telegraph pole burst upwards in an eruption of earth. The vine slumped against the wall, smashing through brick. Hundreds of barbs scraped the brickwork, rasping as they reached for her.

The scene brightened as moonlight finally peeked through the clouds. Its ambience weak yet managing to break through the darkness and roiling shadows.

It highlighted everything.

"Shit!" I shouted.

From the immense trunk, a barb had extended, longer than the others...closer and closer towards Pippa...and it pierced her wrist. Blood trickled.

Her scream filled my head.

Again, I charged forward and again the barrier forced me back. Pathetic sparks dripped from the Witchblade—still the damn thing was useless. Something was draining its energy.

One of the phantoms, her face glistening in the silver light of the moon, pointed to her wrist. The others stroked theirs, too. A few even nodded. Their freaky, faceless heads bobbed up and down in a stuttering blur. Even more grotesque now they were lit up by the moon.

"I can see that!" I shouted. I knew that barb had pierced Pippa's wrist. What did they want me to do?

A phantom shook her head.

"No?" This was insane. But fuck, I should be used to this.

The same phantom slapped her wrist, so hard I almost heard it. Slap-slap-slap-slapslap... No, it wasn't her wrist, but her forearm.

"What?" Then I knew. I knew without a doubt what these dead witches referred to. I pulled back my sleeve to reveal a scar where once I was branded in the shape of the same sigil Pippa had painted.

I shouted at them, my voice a roar: "This?" I held up my arm. The skin itched and burned like fresh sunburn. What precisely were these phantoms telling me?

Pippa still thrashed in the embrace of the shadows and coiled vines. Another barb had pressed into her other wrist, and blood trickled down her hands to drip from clawed fingers. Her clothes were filthy, smeared black with mud and fungus.

At her feet, in front of the slithering vines, the shadows bloomed and opened up.

An image flashed.

I blinked.

The unfolding darkness lightened and wavered like a poor-quality video. Then sharpened, in and out of focus to show something familiar: Pippa's scattered paintings and spilled paints. I watched as I had earlier, the Witchblade—the Witchblade from the *past*—write HELP ME. Only this time a ghostly hand visibly gripped its hilt, the knuckles gnarled and arthritic, liver-spotted and wrinkled. The image panned back to reveal the frail and hunched form of another witch. Her stained clothes, no more than rags bound by frayed rope, were caked in mud, thick like clay. Across thin shoulders draped a dark patchwork shawl, leathery and rumpled. She released the blade and as before, it dropped to the floorboards. The crone stepped back and turned and looked directly at me.

I jerked and coughed, and I hoped to hell I hadn't inhaled any of those spores—although their clouds had calmed now I'd stepped further back.

Tiny eyes, darker than the surrounding shadows, glared through a mass of spider-web hair. Her nose was a fleshy lump above the thin slit of a mouth that curled into a twist of scar tissue. Once upon a time she'd been burned. Badly. I thought of Pippa's market square painting; the one where the witch writhed in roaring flames. Was this her whose form now shimmered as she reached the edge of the shadows? Was this a portal?

The darkness shuddered. She stepped through into the present.

Shadows sucked at her and there she stood. Nettles smouldered and shrivelled, crumbled dead at her feet. Even the earth blackened. Smoke and shadow curled into the air. She lifted her head and eyed the Witchblade in my hand. Her lips twitched, the webbed scar silvering beneath the moonlight. Twitch-twitch, twitch. Was that a smile?

The Witchblade—the Witchblade of the *present*— jerked and a warmth spread up my arm. Traceries of white fire spat from the blade. Still its power was limited. I gripped tighter. The same white energy skittered across the crone's shawl, weaving with the stitches between each patchwork section. It seemed to writhe, charged with new power.

Then it all made sense.

"You crafty bitch," I shouted.

Already having sufficient power to snatch the Witchblade from me in Pippa's studio—somehow twisting time, too—this crone had harnessed its energy.

Leading me here, she'd then channelled the energy so to transport herself from the death, the *hell*, she came. The way her form shifted and shivered, edges fuzzy one moment and sharp the next, suggested this was only part of her resurrection.

Another piece of this puzzle was Pippa.

She was still framed by the great hulks of vine, barbs secured into veins. Waves of shadow braced her shoulders and bound her arms. Her head lolled, her eyelids droopy as though she was drunk. Soft moans drifted towards me.

Seeing her like that made me feel so damn helpless.

The crone, of all the other witches, was undoubtedly the most powerful; evidently the only one present with such power to cheat death, even though she'd been burnt at the stake. Her shawl moved as though the wind was fiercer than it was. A patchwork of fabrics…brown, dark, stained. And it moved, contradicting the crone's own movements as she approached Pippa. It was alive, pulsing. *Breathing.* The darker patches reminded me of the Shadow Fabric, the way it shifted like spilled diesel. The crumpled sections, some kind of animal hide, had been stitched with it.

Then I knew precisely who this crone was. How she'd accomplished all this I hadn't a clue, but I had no doubt of her identity.

Belle Mayher. A woman who was said to have lived beyond the age of 250, noted to have stitched the largest sections of the Shadow Fabric. The very Fabric that would later be unleashed across London in 1666, before the Great Fire. Her powers were unparalleled and included the unique ability to absorb others' powers and abilities. She had been—still was?—in league with an entity known as Clay, Demon Stitcher of Shadow and Skin. Human skin, not animal hide (to demons we *are* animals). Selling your soul was not a myth; she'd done precisely that. And she wore proof to the fact.

I could only assume she was at this very moment absorbing Pippa's artistic skills. To what gains, I had no idea. I knew for certain, however, she was even now absorbing the Witchblade energy; that's why its power was weak.

A cold wind bit through my clothes and I shivered.

The other phantoms had retreated. Some huddled against each other. The one with the baby shook uncontrollably. Fungus grew from the rags she cradled. The closest phantom whose feet dripped dark water, frantically waved her forearm and it was as if I heard her yell for my attention…even though she had no mouth. She made sawing motions across her forearm.

Was she telling me to cut myself?

I raised the Witchblade.

She stopped sawing and her faceless head jerked in affirmation. Dark splashes flicked upwards.

I didn't want to cut myself, that was absurd. My scar, shaped like an hourglass, had become part of me and this dead witch wanted me to cut it. Not a day had passed when I didn't drag my fingertips over the lumpy twists of skin, thinking, remembering… I guessed I'd always be connected to the darkness that we humans are so ignorant towards. It's always been there, and always will be.

The crone, Mayher, had grasped Pippa's head in one hand and a barbed vine in the other. Blood gushed from her serrated palm. Her lips moved, chanting some witchcraft bullshit. Her shawl surged and writhed about her shoulders, energised.

Moonlight reflected from the blade I held before me. I could only guess that cutting myself would somehow reenergise the Witchblade, to steal the power back from Mayher. I pressed it, warm, vibrating, against the scar and quickly sliced along the outer edge of the sigil.

A thin line blossomed red, oozing. Entirely painless.

From across the ruins, the crone's dark gaze struck me. My hand froze. Her lips peeled back over broken teeth and she hissed louder than the wind.

Now I bled, having done what I'd been instructed—advised by a dead witch, for God's sake—what the hell was I supposed to do now?

I lifted my arm and shook it.

Blood spattered and disappeared onto the blackened ground.

The fungus quivered, the grey heads lightening, breaking apart. I waved my arm around, the blood pouring out—worryingly a little more than I'd hoped. But it worked. The fungus shrivelled and crumbled. Swiftly, quicker than I would've expected, the clumps dissolved. The air no longer tasted as tainted as before, and I stepped forward over the dead ground. Blood dripped down my forearm, my fingers now slick.

Pippa's body no longer moved. I hoped I wasn't too late.

The shadows had even retreated.

"Ha!" I yelled into the swirling masses as they drifted away.

I ran towards Pippa and Mayher. Fungus puffed into harmless dust beneath my pounding boots. The nettles and brambles and grass broke away with the crumbling fungus, leaving dead ground, mud and dirt.

The crone's scar twisted ugly and she glared at me, eyes a wicked Stygian darkness. Her shawl seethed around her shoulders, the patches squirming and glistening. She shrieked.

It drilled into my brain and I staggered. Colourful zigzags pressed in on my vision, threatening to yank me into the shrivelled tangles of blackened nettles and grass. Witchblade fire spat and charged, red and orange and yellow flares lit my way. Finally, I had control; I had the blade's power back in hand. My muscles flexed and I straightened.

Still Mayher shrieked, hunched and buckled over as the faint energy drifted across her shoulders and down to clawed hands. White charges spat from her fingertips. She'd lost control of that stolen power.

I leapt and booted her in the chest.

My foot passed through her…but slammed into the shawl. It flew from her and slapped the brickwork. It fell, twitching in the still-dissolving fungus.

Mayher staggered backwards as though I'd succeeded in kicking her. Her ephemeral form shifted and slid from focus, merging and churning with the broiling darkness. Her shriek was now dampened, subdued by the retreating shadows. Through weak, grey eyes she looked down at her shawl.

Part-flesh, part-shadow, the foul garment writhed on the ground. Patchwork sections had come undone and the flesh seethed, rippled. Blood oozed from torn stitches, and frayed ends of shadow squirmed as though desperate to be threaded once more.

Defying the shadows that embraced her, Mayher rushed for me. The darkness shredded.

She yelled and swiped at me.

I crouched and swung my arm up to block, ready to thrust with the Witchblade. Her gnarled fingers passed through me.

Hair rose on the back of my neck.

Behind her, the darkness thickened. Dense tendrils whipped around her neck and torso to snatch her backwards, her heels digging into the ground yet leaving no mark. Her eyes flared. The shadows were determined to take her back into death. She struggled, throwing glances at her shawl that bled into the cracked earth.

Pippa still hadn't moved. Still the barbs were rooted in her veins. The shadows that bound her wrists drifted away yet the vine held her upright. They hadn't dissolved with the rest of the fungus. Being as trunk-like as they were, I guessed they'd be the last to respond to whatever power my blood contained. This was new to me; all this was a different kind of weird.

I reached Pippa and stabbed those massive trunks. Witchblade fire, white and brilliant, rushed towards the barbs that punctured her skin. Black filth bubbled and oozed from the wounds and the barbs slid free. Harmless to us, the fire roared and enveloped the trunks. The thick flesh blistered, stinking and smouldering. They thumped the ground and deflated, shrivelling into twisted coils of muck.

Pippa flopped into my arms. I propped her against the wall. Her eyelids flickered and she murmured something.

Mayhar's scream pulled me upright.

The phantoms were all now animated, their faceless heads turned to the crone as she kicked at the shadows. The other witches were clearly fearful of Mayher which led me to believe she'd somehow collected them here to reinforce her resurrection. I could only assume she'd absorbed their abilities and crafts even in death.

Mayher had somehow reached her shawl, now clutching its patchwork remains together. Gore dripped from it in clumps, black threads dangling.

I jumped up. Witchblade fire erupted from the blade and I rushed towards her as again she attempted to strike me. A darkness flickered behind her eyes as though energised once again by the shawl. White energy flared from the blade and shot into her face. Again, this witch burned. 350 years beyond her death, after a failed resurrection, fire ate into her skin once again; Witchblade fire she failed to control.

Her scream tore through the countryside.

I swiped the blade downwards into the shawl. It sliced through the fabric. Shadows bubbled and flesh bled. The crone retreated. She flailed, desperate to hold on to the garment. Again the shadows snatched at her.

Pippa was pushing herself to unsteady feet.

"Go!" I shouted at her.

She scrubbed the blood and filth from her arms and succeeded only in smearing it. Her hair obscured her face.

The shadows were diminishing, and the fungus shrank to become little more than grey goo. So too were the remaining vines, crumbling to dust.

The phantoms whipped the shadows into clouds and as one, they swarmed Mayher. A blur of ghostly rags and skinny limbs flew down on the crone. Glimmers of faces, eyes and noses and mouths appeared—some of them were attractive, or had been in their day. Pretty faces, whether innocent of witchcraft, whether practitioners of white or black arts, they had been released. No longer were they the forgotten faces of the 17th-century witch trials.

Mayher struggled beneath the onslaught of phantoms and deeper shadows that surged around them all. A wall shook and collapsed in a rush of brick dust and lingering shadow. I had no idea what the ground would do given that the fungus was shrivelling and the vines crumbled.

"Run!" That word had become too familiar. Ever since the evil behind the shadows had returned, ever since the hell that had occurred at Periwick House, I'd shouted that a lot.

So we ran. With a final glance over my shoulder I saw Mayher and the phantoms vanish in a vortex of shadow.

Moonlight swamped the area, cleaner, fresher. A dust cloud caught on the wind.

We sprinted across the fields. When we were safe, I looked at Pippa.

Just like the phantoms, she had no face.

Editor's Note: Turnabout is fair play, but even more the "Witchblade" was introduced in a story, "Ten Minutes Till Deadtime" in *Hell's Garden: Mad, Bad, and Ghostly Gardeners*, which I also edited. When this story was offered, I jumped at it.

Mark Cassell lives in a rural part of the UK with his wife and a number of animals. He often dreams of dystopian futures, peculiar creatures, and flitting shadows. Primarily a horror writer, his steampunk, dark fantasy, and SF stories have featured in several anthologies and ezines. His latest release, *Sinister Stitches,* is a collection of stories from a mythos that began with his debut novel, *The Shadow Fabric*, a supernatural horror tale of demons, devices, and deceit.

For more about Mark and his work, or to contact him directly:

Twitter: @Mark_Cassell

Facebook: www.facebook.com/AuthorMarkCassell

Blog: www.beneath.co.uk

The Shadow Fabric mythos: www.theshadowfabric.co.uk

Newsletter: www.markcassell.com

To Thine Self Be True was inspired by the 1974 novel, The Sentinel, by Jeffrey Konvitz.

To Thine Self Be True
By Alp Beck

"What do you think, Liz? Should we take it?" Greg looked at his wife, hopefully.

"Doesn't the price seem a little too low? Too good to be true?" Liz toyed with the hair of her troll doll key chain; a sure sign she was worried. "You know what my dad says, "If it's too good—""

"Yeah, I know. For God's sake, please stop quoting your father every chance you get. You married me, you know, not him." Why did she constantly have to bring up his freaking father-in-law? "You heard the agent, it's because the house comes with a tenant. That's a good thing, as far as I'm concerned: built-in income."

Greg didn't even know how much rent the tenant was paying, that was part of the contract. The real estate agent was very specific; he was not to ask. Whatever it was, it was worth it. The house was an incredible steal, especially in this neighborhood.

"C'mon, honey. We'll never get a deal like this again. Have you seen this house? Do you know where we are?" Liz looked at him. She could see the hunger his eyes, his desperate need to impress her father, so she relented.

179

"Okay."

"Yes!" Greg grabbed Liz and squeezed her in a bear hug. Then he turned to the agent. "Lady, you've got yourself a sale!"

Greg stood in the middle of the kitchen looking up at the ceiling, then he looked down at the rent check in his hand from the Hekate Society: a company that didn't exist—according to Google; a measly 102 dollars. Two years into their homeownership and they still hadn't found a way to get the old lady out of there. It didn't bother Liz since she felt their mortgage payment was low enough that they didn't need the extra cash, but Greg had other ideas. He wanted the old woman out. He knew he could make a fortune in rent from that apartment; even though he'd never even seen it. It had to be at least as large as the first floor, and that was plenty big.

The whole situation upstairs was weird.

Once a week, some big guy delivered stuff—groceries, he supposed—to her apartment. He probably had a key. Something that enraged him, since they were the owners of the damn house, and they didn't have a key!

To this day, he'd never laid eyes on the woman. Quiet as a mouse. Every so often, late at night, he'd hear some scuffling coming from upstairs, like she was wrestling someone. And, what kind of a name was Chelleach? There it was on the check, plain as day: RENT — FOR CHELLEACH MORRIGAN. He had not figured out how yet, but he was going to get that woman out of here, one way or another, no matter what Liz, or that damn contract, said.

Liz looked at the garbage piled by the front door. It was Greg's job to take it out twice a week and put it by the curb. But it seemed, of late, he wasn't interested in doing much of anything. He left early and came home late. She'd been patient. She had not mentioned how she was beginning to feel disconnected; how he just came home and turned on the TV. She didn't talk about the liquor on his breath, or the way he stank of cigarette smoke, even though he'd quit three years earlier.

She grabbed the five bags of trash and clumsily made her way out the door. As soon as she did, the door shut behind her. In a panic, she realized the door was set to auto-lock and she didn't have another set of keys hidden. Greg had taken the spare set to work with him months ago. When he lost his, he'd never replaced them.

"Ciallaionn se a gortaitear thu."

Liz looked up, startled. Her tenant stood at the top of the stairs. White hair crowned her head and cascaded down her shoulders stopping halfway down her body. Granted, she was quite short, but still the effect was that of a snow-capped mountain. The luminescence of her hair was so intense that it seemed to light the darkness around her. Deep-set, piercing, blue eyes looked out of a face so craggy with lines, that it might have been grown out of tree bark.

"Ciallaionn se a gortaitear thu."

"What?" Liz said.

Chelleach just stared intensely, as if willing Liz to read her mind.

"I don't understand—"

The old woman just harrumphed in evident frustration. Then she tossed something, small and silvery, at her feet. Liz looked down and was amazed to see it was a key. She glanced up, ready to thank her, but she was already gone. Sighing, she turned to her door and tried the key. It fit perfectly. She let herself in and tossed the garbage bags where they had been earlier. Let Greg deal with them. Instead, she ran to her laptop and opened Google translate, making sure she had 'Detect Language Automatically' set. She typed the phrase phonetically, as best as she could remember it, and hit Enter. Google spit out the translation.

'He means to hurt thou' and it was Gaelic.

Greg stumbled in, stinking of booze and sweat. Liz startled awake. She sneaked a glance at the wall clock: 1:00 A.M. and he was just getting home; the third time this week. She got up off the couch, still not fully awake.

"Don't you dare say a thing." Greg snarled, as he tossed his jacket on the back of a chair. He'd been fired from his job at the bank earlier this week and had not yet told Liz. Idiots. Saying that he was not a team player and that he made people nervous with his confrontational style. Screw 'em, he'd show them all, the bastards.

Liz took a breath before speaking.

"Greg—"

"What! What are you going to say?" Spittle flew as he shouted. "The same old bullshit?" His eyes were mean. "I knew you would be here," he said mockingly. "Looking for something to tell your daddy; how I screwed up and am not as good as him. Just looking to get on my freaking back. If you've got nothing good to say, just shut the hell up and leave me alone!" He knew none of this was Liz's fault, but he just couldn't control himself. He felt the anger coming off him in waves and didn't care. Time to blow off some steam.

"Greg—" Liz tried again. Greg advanced on her fast, until he was an inch from her face.

"I. Said. Shut. Up!" He raised his fist, threateningly. Liz backed up, alarmed, forgetting the basement steps were right behind her.

Too late she realized her misstep. She lost her balance and fell back.

Greg watched in horror as his wife tumbled backwards, her arms flailing uselessly for a second, as she tried to find purchase. Everything happened in slow motion: Her arms reached for him. His hand touched only the tips of her fingers—out of his grasp in a millisecond. Her body trying to right itself, almost making it, then failing as she plunged downward. The shape of her mouth transformed into a startled "O" as she realized what was happening; the horrible crack her head made as it hit one of the concrete steps, her body catapulting, feet over head, not stopping until landing on the basement floor.

He shouted her name, taking the stairs two at a time, until he was next to her. He knelt beside her. Her head was bleeding and one of her legs was bent at a 90 degree angle. She was unconscious.

He grabbed for his phone to call 911, then realized it was still in his jacket pocket upstairs. He ran up the stairs and that's when he saw it—the melted candles, the porterhouse steak in the platter, sliced the way he liked it, the fresh mashed potatoes beside it—his favorite meal—and in his plate sat a little, yellow onesie with the words, 'Nine Months 'till I Meet You, Daddy!'

In the distance an inhuman keening sounded, muffled by the roar in his head, like that of an angry river. He thought he saw movement in the corner of the room, a flash of white flowing hair, and then it was gone.

The wail was his own.

For a couple of years, after the loss of their baby, things settled down. Greg was attentive and kind again and Liz recuperated at home. He found another job, this one at a bottling plant. He and Liz found solace in each other. She didn't hold him responsible for the fall, even though he did. They were sad for a while but took comfort in the fact that they could try again. No permanent damage, the doctors had said. He stopped drinking. Got himself into AA. Made the meetings and took stock of his life. He was determined to make good on his resolve. He would never let things get so out of control.

Liz's father paid for a nurse to stay with them and help with Liz's recovery. Greg resisted the urge to toss the woman out. His father-in-law seemed to enjoy throwing his wealth in Greg's face. Greg pushed all the resentment down. He wasn't that man anymore. He looked down at the Alcoholics Anonymous, 2-year sober chip, never far from him. 'To Thine Self Be True'

Yeah. He had plans, big plans. He'd show them all.

"So you're sure about this?" Greg asked Dan.

Dan was a recent hire at the plant. They had become buddies the day Dan had covered for Greg's lateness by punching in Greg's time card. He had done this without being asked or even knowing Greg that well.

After a while, they began taking their lunches together. Greg discovered that they were very much alike. They were both hungry and wanted more from life. They would spend time talking about getting more money, finding opportunities, outrageous scams and what they'd spend their fortune on, once they had it.

"Yeah. I'm telling you, this will make us both rich." Dan said.

"Tell me again, how this works?"

"We go in, 50/50, on a vending route. I have a friend who is selling his. All we need is forty grand to buy it. We'll make money from day one. It's a guaranteed, profitable route. He's retiring to Boca Raton."

"Forty thousand? You sure he won't take any less? That's an awful lot of money."

"Yeah. No discounts. The route is a moneymaker. But you only have to come up with twenty, since I have the other half."

Greg had gone over this in his mind, numerous times. All they had in the bank was the twenty thousand that his in-laws had given them on their wedding day. But if he did this, it would be for Liz and their baby; for their future.

"Okay. I'm in." Dan jumped up and high-fived him.

"Yes! Millionaire's Club, here we come!" Then he looked at Greg. "Don't forget. My buddy wants cash. He wants to keep the IRS' greedy fingers out of his pockets."

"Yeah. Yeah. I got it."

The next day, Greg brought the cash in an envelope, and stashed it in his locker. Later, they would meet with Dan's friend and close the deal. He could almost taste freedom and it was green.

Dan didn't come to work that day so Greg left him a couple of messages to make sure he was okay. At the end of his shift he went to his locker. When he opened it, the envelope was gone. He frantically emptied everything from the cabinet, not caring where stuff landed.

"No... no... no... NOOOOOO!" He screamed as he banged his fists against the metal.

Nope. No envelope. As if it had never been there.

He had been duped.

It took three security personnel to calm him down and then his boss sent him home.

He left and turned into the nearest pub.

Liz got up slowly from the bed. Her ribs hurt and her arms were covered in small bruises, where Greg had pinched her. He'd grown very fond of his little game. If she didn't get him his beer quickly enough, or displeased him in some way, he'd pinch her somewhere hard, then laugh uproariously as if it were a big joke. Then he'd kiss her and slap her bottom. "It's all in love, sweetie. All in love." He made sure never to pinch her somewhere the marks could be seen, but just in case, he always demanded she wear long sleeved blouses when dining with her parents.

The last few times, he started really hitting her. Punches, kicks, all were fair game. He didn't even need a reason anymore.

She checked herself. Nothing seemed to be broken, but she sure did hurt this morning.

Greg had come home in a nasty mood again; drunk and mean. She'd asked him how his day had been and he'd gone off, bellowing that now he was officially laid off from the plant.

"It's temporary, they said. But, oh, I know better. Asses, every last one of them!" He ranted and paced the room wildly, like a caged lion.

She's made the mistake of mentioning that maybe they'd hire him back soon. It was only temporary. At that, he'd frozen in place. This scared her more than the frantic pacing. She'd looked into his eyes, and seen the glassy, meanness in them.

"Oh? What the hell do you know about it?"

That's when he punched her, hard enough to make her vomit. Once she fell, he started kicking. That was the last thing she remembered.

He wasn't home. Good. He was out doing God knows what. She didn't even care anymore. He'd worn her down. He had become what her parents had warned her about. She was not even angry, or sad. Worse, she was indifferent. Everything was gray. No highs. No lows.

She gingerly put on her bathrobe and made her way to the front door to get the mail. When she opened it, she saw a small basket sitting there. She bent down, picked it up and brought it to the kitchen table. Inside was an old fashioned bag of ice, like you saw in old cartoons, and a little glass jar filled with some green and phosphorescent unguent. She opened it, and her eyes began to tear immediately at the pungent smell. She looked at the front of the jar and saw only two words handwritten on a yellowed label:

FOR PAIN.

Puzzled, she took the jar to the bathroom vanity. She opened her robe and raised her pajama top. Gently, she applied some of the concoction to the section that hurt the most. Miraculously, the pain disappeared immediately. She then smiled for the first time in months.

Liz stood in front of the apartment door and nervously knocked. She didn't think she'd get an answer. She'd tried at other times. C, as Liz referred to her — because, who could pronounce that name? — never opened the door. Other than the time she had locked herself out, she had never seen her again. Greg had tried to get her out. He'd blasted the stereo system, with never ending acid rock. He'd sneak mice under her door, knowing full well that they would invade the entire house. That never happened. They had simply disappeared.

He'd shut off the heat and electricity to her apartment, in spite of her begging him not to. But nothing had come of it. No response was had. Liz reminded Greg daily of the contract they had signed: they were not to evict the tenant, or do anything to jeopardize her living quarters. And yet, he persisted. After a while, Liz just did not care. Her monochrome world made that possible.

Now, here she was. Trying again. She had a need to thank the old woman. Her balm had not only made the pain vanish, it had awakened her from her catatonia. Life now had color.

She knocked again. This time the door opened when her knuckles made contact with the wood.

"Hello?" She pushed on the door gently, widening the gap.

"Hello? Is anyone there?" She walked into the darkness, using the wall as a guide.

As soon as she disappeared fully into the apartment, the door slammed shut behind her.

Greg walked into the house slowly. The front door was open. All the shades were up and the house was dark. The glow of the TV was the only light in the kitchen and Liz was nowhere to be seen.

"Liz? Honey?" Nothing. No Liz. Where the hell was she? She was supposed to have dinner ready for him, she knew that. He turned on the overhead light.

Nothing. Weird.

"Liz? Stop fooling around, you know I don't like games." He walked into the bedroom. The bed was unmade. Liz always made the bed. The glow of the streetlight cast odd shadows into the room. He turned on the bedside lamp...

...and jumped.

Liz sat in the corner wing chair.

Unmoving.

"Liz, what the hell are you doing?" Something was not right. A chill ran through him.

She didn't respond. She looked off into the distance.

Past him.

Behind him.

He turned. A smallish, wrinkled woman, stood there. She had the whitest hair he'd ever seen; so white, in fact, it seemed to glow. Her glacier-blue gaze froze his body in place. He gasped and began to pant without knowing why. He blinked and tried to shake off the ice building in his veins. The old woman smiled a dark toothless smile, fathomless and deep. It widened past her face, impossibly large. Then, she grabbed his wrist with a cold, parchment-like grip and, with a quick twist she snapped it. That broke his paralysis. He screamed then for all he was worth and her smile widened. With her other hand, she grabbed the same arm, further up, and shattered it. He watched in disbelief. She continued traveling up his arm, her grip unshakable, continuously breaking the bone as she moved. She switched to his other arm and began the same process. Greg collapsed. His bladder emptied and he felt himself fade, but he refused to surrender to the impossibility of this moment. This could NOT be happening. He would not let it. He struggled against her grip, trying to escape. She grabbed his ankle then and snapped it in two. Mercifully the pain won and he passed out.

The old woman continued to methodically break his bones; first one leg, then the other. Then the neck, the torso and the hips. She folded the various parts as she went. Nothing hampered her progress. She saved the head for last, imploding it with a swift heel to the nose until Greg's corpse was nothing more than an indistinguishable mass of bloodied bone, muscle and tissue.

Liz stood up then. Chelleach waited. She made her way to where the old woman stood. She leaned in and embraced her, feeling the weight of her in her arms. Chelleach let herself go. The longer she held her, the more insubstantial she became until only Liz remained and no other.

Then Liz slowly made her way up the stairs, feeling her age, as she entered her apartment and closed the door.

The young couple roamed around the house. It was the sixth one they had looked at today and, incredibly, it was exactly what they were looking for; within their price range. They could not believe their luck.

Mike turned to the real estate agent, his pretty, young wife doing a poor job of hiding her excitement.

"Okay, this house seems to fit all our criteria," said Mike. "So, what don't I know?" He was naturally suspicious and his gut told him the price was too good to be true. These real estate people were always taking advantage of dupes. They were no better than used car dealers.

"Ah, yes. There is one condition to buying this house." The agent smiled a predatory smile. "It comes with a tenant."

Alp Beck was raised in Italy and Cuba, the product of a brilliant Italian artist/actress and a talented Cuban opera singer. She writes in all mediums but prefers horror; she has had essays published in the *NY Times* and the *NY Blade*. Her upcoming novella, *Fresh*, will be coming out in 2016. She is hard at work on a series of short stories, including "Eyewitness" (release date 2016) and "The Underride," a project with her co-writer, Laurie Jones.

http://twitter.com/Alphorizons
www.alphorizons.com

If you enjoyed the works of these wonderful writers, please do use the links to let them know or leave a review at your retailer.

Other Works by April Grey

Six talented writers explore the various paths Evil can take when in Hell's Garden. Featuring tales by Rayne Hall, Heather Holland Wheaton, Jonathan Broughton, Mark Cassell, Eric Dimbleby and Jeff Hargett. Edited by April Grey.

The Fairy
Cake Bake Shoppe
And 13 Other Weird Tales

April Grey

Sexbots threaten to destroy a marriage. A half-alien embryo remains the only hope for the human race. Tempting cupcakes that aren't just bad for your waistline, but may result in permanent injury. Welcome to the realm of April Grey. Steampunk Zombies, The HG Avenger, Nefarious Chihuahuas, Lothario Dolphins, and many other bizarre characters lurk in these short stories.

What is love? In the eye of the beholder or something more? In these four dark tales, zombies, ghosts, ancient spells and modern crooks show us that love conquers all--even death and despair. Includes I'll Love You Forever, The Vision, and stories from Troll Bridge.

One Man, Two Women, Two Gods...who will survive the Trickster's snare? Ghostly images materialize in Nina Weaver's photos. Goons try to kidnap her. When her photographs are stolen and her best friend is shot, she realizes that she has no one to turn to but her ex-lover, Pascal "Goofy" Guzman. Together they go on a desperate road trip in search of answers. The truth is darker and more terrifying than Nina could ever have imagined. After their love re-ignites, they fall into the Trickster God's trap.

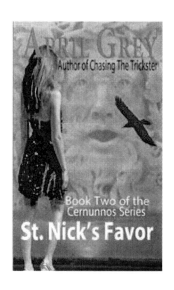

St. Nicholas asks Nina Weaver to be his emissary. Her mission is to take a one-way trip five years into her past to save the lives of thousands of children. Doing this will result in her losing the life she has built in New York City, including her relationship with Pascal Guzman. Nina faces down corporate greed, attempts on her life and the terrors of the Trickster God to keep her promise.

CPSIA information can be obtained at www.ICGtesting.com
Printed in the USA
LVOW07s1252210116

471664LV00031B/14/P

9 781523 261635